BIRTHSTONES

BIRTHSTONES

by

Phyllis Gotlieb

Afterword by Nalo Hopkinson

Robert J.
SAWYER
BOOKS

Robert J. Sawyer Books
Published by Red Deer Press, A Fitzhenry & Whiteside Company
1512, 1800–4 Street S.W., Calgary, Alberta, Canada t2s 2s5 • www.reddeerpress.com

Credits
Edited for the Press by Robert J. Sawyer
Copyedited by Chris Szego
Cover and text design by Karen Petherick Thomas
Cover image courtesy Shutterstock.com/Nguyen Thai
Printed and bound in Canada by Friesens for Red Deer Press

Acknowledgments
Financial support provided by the Canada Council, and the Government of Canada through the Book Publishing Industry Development Program (BPIDP).

Canada Council   Conseil des Arts
for the Arts   du Canada

Library and Archives Canada Cataloguing in Publication
Gotlieb, Phyllis, 1926-
      Birthstones / Phyllis Gotlieb.
ISBN 978-0-88995-390-1 (bound)   ISBN 978-0-88995-385-7 (pbk.)
      I. Title.
PS8513.O7B47 2007   C813'.54   C2007-900258-7

United States Cataloguing-in-Publication Data
Gotleib, Phyllis, 1926-
   Birthstones / Phyllis Gotleib.
[224] p. : cm.
Summary: On a dark and moonless planet, mutations have left women as little more than wombs, while men can teleport but have limited control over the ability. When aliens come to plunder this world's resources, the already harsh environment degrades exponentially.
ISBN-13: 978-0-88995-390-1   ISBN-10: 0-88995-390-2
ISBN-13: 978-0-88995-385-7 (pbk.)   ISBN-10: 0-88995-385-6 (pbk.)
1. Science fiction. 2. Woman—Fiction. I. Title.
813/.54 dc22   PR9199.3.G685.B5 2007

DEDICATION

In memory of Professor John D. Robins
Victoria College, University of Toronto

BIRTHSTONES

* * O N E * *

THE WORLD SHAR:

CAPITAL CITY OF THE EQUATORIAL LANDS

On the world Shar the skies were dark ochre and the sun was red at noon. Of all the countries of the world, the Equatorial Lands was the greatest, and included a continent crisscrossed with broad and salty rivers, and surrounded by thousands of islands and peninsulas. Its greatest city had been named Aesh's-Land after the first emperor, and its country was the richest for the growing of crops in an otherwise largely barren world.

In the capital city at this hot noon the present Emperor of the Lands, Aesh Seven, stood waiting, along with the members of his Council, and three representatives of Galactic Federation, in the largest of the Birthing Centers.

Its pointed roof rose out of a cluster of low buildings, six-sided like them and tiled in the same deep ochre. Their color was just lighter than the ground, slightly darker than the sky.

Inside, through the tall windows, shafts of the red sunlight lit the dancing insects, and the motes of the dusty air; but the walls were also lit with fluorescent tubes, a rare touch of technology on a world that scarcely needed warmth and could not bear more pollution. The air was still and silent.

A woman was about to give birth. Not quite woman.

And not quite Emperor; the term was an ancient one on Shar, and its meaning these days was closer to chieftain, and Aesh Seven was elected by his Council. He stood among them, one of forty men in sleeveless leather tunics, the guardhairs of his dark fur picking out thin lights from the lamps. His clawed feet were set in leather clogs and there was no other movement in him; only his eyes, like pomegranate seeds swimming in red membranes, flickered occasionally, and his clawed fingers tightened on his staff.

Before him stood the most important Shar in the world at this moment, the attending birther, who had no important tunic to wear, but stood naked, like the child he would deliver. The vestigial webbing in his armpits unfolded and folded back as he dipped his hands into the basin where the female, not-woman, limbless mutant lay, swollen with the unborn.

Near the opposite walls of the room were thirty-odd other basins with these inhabitants, impregnated joylessly by men of Shar, bearing fetuses in various stages of development. There were no other women except these womb-capsules on this polluted world.

The birther's hands reached into the womb's entrance, sought for and found the emerging child and plucked it out easily: a whole-limbed male, as verified by Galactic Federation scientists; otherwise this birth would not have been chosen for the ceremony.

The child coughed, weakly at first, and began to whimper. A tiny creature, glistening with liquids, minuscule fists clenched and trembling, sharp ears twitching in time with the bit of a quivering tail shaped like the ace of spades.

The birther knotted off the umbilicus and delivered it to the Emperor's representative, Kohav, waiting with a blanket. He wrapped it and presented the hairy bundle to the taller of the two Earthers, Genever, the Envoy of Galactic Federation, who was sweating along with his associates in stiff and sober cloth.

"Take," the birther said in a hoarse whisper.

In acceptance of this trust Genever bent and clutched it, a mere double handful in his big pink hands. Delius, the aide standing beside him, did not bother glancing at his impassive diplomat's face. It did not matter whether Genever was worried about having his clothes, dark blue with gold frogs, spattered, or whatever else he might be thinking. The Shar are not at all telepathic, and anyway Genever had a subdermal impervious helmet.

The Emperor struck the brick floor with his staff: *Yes!* As if Genever had passed an undeclared test.

The child's whimper burst into a squall, and the Envoy handed it to Delius, who jigged it gently, as he used to do with his own infant son. But the birther quickly grasped it from him and placed it in the Emperor's hands.

Aesh Seven raised it as a gift to his people, and cried out, "Here is the father of our hope!" once in his own language and once in Galactic *lingua*, then placed it on the belly of its unknowing bearer to suckle on one of the three swollen teats. Delius fought to keep himself from shivering, and was not sorry that none but local media had been allowed here.

Now the Envoy presented the Emperor with a document sealed in a red leather case with gold stamping, and spoke in the Emperor's own tongue: "We will bring you true mothers for your children, help you beget whole ones of your own, and make your world clean. We swear it and this is our sign and seal." He was well practised in these phrases. Delius was ready to cue him if he forgot.

The sound of clattering made Delius glance through an opened doorway and he realized that a crowd had gathered outside the metal railings that fenced the building; their faces were impassive, but those who carried staffs or canes had raised and were clacking them with those of their neighbors in applause.

Aesh Seven then cried out in his hoarse voice, "So you agree now, do you, citizens?" and did not wait for an answer or seem to notice that there were those who only leaned on their staffs.

Delius knew that Aesh had declared a holiday. And what did these men do on working days, then? He doubted they had any well-paying employment among the aliens who owned the world, the outworld corporations who lived and worked in the orbiting city of offices and warehouses, giving orders to the crews controlling the robots that dug, the satellites that surveyed, and the factories that refined the riches of the world below. The Shar people had not been built for such work, with their slender limbs and bent-kneed stance, though they were strong and wiry enough for their own enterprises.

But what work, then? Tenders of those womb-bearers, mainly, half their population. Servile without choice to others—who descended only to inspect their fiefdoms—in the manner of tribes caught in the whirlpools of "civilization." Out-worlders were a bit contemptuous of Shar, and also a bit frightened.

One of those who had not raised a staff lifted it now, and howled through the black O of his mouth words that needed no translation, "Not all of us want these damned aliens!" Crashing his staff against the railing so that it broke in two, "Are there not enough of them eating us up already?"

His eyes flashed, his body with raised arms became a black X of shadow and was—

—nothing—

—then solidly less than half a meter away from Genever, with its oily sweat and strangely sweet breath, with its hint of cloves, that bypassed the Earthers' nose filters. Delius's arm shot out across the Shar's body to stop him and he fell back, his comrades grasped him and hid him among themselves.

The Shar people are the only known teleports. That is what makes them frightening.

Genever blinked and gasped, but immediately smoothed down.

Aesh Seven jumped forward snarling with bared fangs: "Find me that one!"

But before any of his attendants could move, Delius bowed and made a gesture of beseechment with hands clasped: "If you please, my lord—"

And Kohav stepped forward and said, "My lord, it is your holiday…"

After that, with the help of Kohav, Genever and Delius performed the small drama of persuading the Emperor not to mar that holiday. Aesh knew well enough that Shar cannot control teleportation; it is their reaction to fear and anger.

The afternoon winds were beginning to shiver through the doorways in prelude to the evening storm, and Aesh calmed himself. "Yes, it is the holiday. Let us serve out the meal then, and eat it." And the servants began to set up screens around the containers of the wombs. The day moved quickly in its orbit after that.

꽃

Delius was relieved to be out of there, in the cool stone chamber of their quarters in the Outworld Center that was attached to the Council complex. He was bored with that smooth simpering Genever and weary; the nose filters clogged quickly, mouth breathing irritated and clogged his throat, and he had never been comfortable with the oxycap socket behind his ear. Or, for that matter, in the stiff cloth of his uniform, a grey one to show that he was a rank below Genever. He didn't much care for the chunks of prepared stuff outworlders were forced to eat on strange worlds, but he was used to them. In symbo*lingua* they were all labelled XANTHROTEK. The deep pharmaceutical source of the money.

There were a few conveniences in these quarters: woven mats of the kind Shar slept on, with paddings added for the comfort of aliens; the rest were provided by the Earther prep teams through the same financial source: self-contained plumbing for washing and toilets, sealed jugs of distilled water for drinking, more fluorescent lighting, and packaged food. Also a power-celled air filter, so that Delius could clear his nose for now. He was obliged to share the lodging with Genever, his fellow-Earther; the third outworlder, a Bimanda named Makkow, who managed the archives, was a hermaphrodite in male phase for this assignment, and had a room of his own, with his own world's supplies.

Genever, unlike Delius, was contented, just smoothing his gray-winged hair. He was always placid and smiling. He had hooked in his ear comm and was giving his report to the orbiting GalFed ship. Delius listened in.

"No, no trouble … but then it's all gesture. There are some who don't agree, but their ruler seems to have them in hand."

"They're a weird lot, especially with that jumping."

"There are weirder."

"What about the Polar Territories?"

"Treaties hundreds of years old, never been broken."

"Nothing much worth breaking there, I guess, poor juddars. We'll have the teams down there in two days, start handling the business end and collect you. Off now."

Delius was uneasy as Genever was unruffled. "We don't know how many of those rebels there are." *And can we give them what we promised?* Delius asked the silence.

Genever beamed down on him kindly. "Delius, I've never seen any-one more anxious than you. We've done the task we came for and the matter is settled. And it's quite an iron bar of an arm you have there, the way you handled that violent one."

Delius smiled thinly. He had narrow shoulders with hard muscle on them and his build was deceiving. "I need it to keep people like you safe, Genever…"

"And his number two, Kohav, is a help."

Delius agreed with that. "But none of us really knows what we're in for."

Genever could move quickly when he wanted, and was already

zipped into his sleepsuit and arranging himself on his pallet. "Others will handle that, others…" Muttering now, "You do too damned much deep thinking, Delius, too much…" And falling into a nest of sleep.

Delius switched off the glaring fluorescents, but stayed awake for a long time. Although he was bored with Genever it was not because the man was stupid. Far from it: he sensed, by subtle hints in his manner, that Genever realized that Delius was the kind of Federation agent who reported to others beside himself. Not any kind of spy: code-cracker, recruiter, traitor. Nothing to do with secrets.

Delius had gone into Galactic Service to see worlds, to use his quick eye and restless mind. After long training he had become a Galactic Federation Observer, travelling alone to judge the health of colonies on the worlds chosen for them. When they were in danger of annihilation by unforeseen disasters, his task was pleading, persuading, begging them to move away. Facing angry settlers who could not, would not see the apocalypse coming, he was lucky to escape their fury with a whole skin. The dead judged him in his dreams.

Enough of this emotional battering among all those worlds and their time zones, and he reached a point where he was no longer sure how old he was, or whether there was anyone alive who knew him.

When he was on the verge of burnout his superiors had promoted him into the Entry Corps that forged the first links in the chains of agreements between worlds. The task was essentially the same: he was a guardian of people under risk, with his "iron bar of an arm". But now he had support—not much counting on Genever—and he was no longer alone.

Then he had found a wife, had a child and believed he was satisfied. Or perhaps safe?

Here now was a world of horribly vulnerable people. Men who had been forced to deliver their emotions only to other men. Some longed bitterly for women and others had resigned themselves to having no choices. Some preferred the closeness of men. Now there were teams coming, trying to help coax tax money out of the owners of the mines and factories to clean up the pollution they had intensified by exploiting the resources. After that there would be biology teams working to revitalize the gene pool—and the whole social structure.

More strangers, more interference, and he was beginning to have the same feelings about the Shar that bothered him as an observer of colonists: Watch out! If you don't have enough of them now, there are more Forces coming to take you under control, split you apart! *As I did for all those years.* He knew these thoughts were irrational. *And anyway, Delius, when did you ever dare think you had any power?* Finally he fell asleep, and found himself swimming in the dream of a womb. He broke out of that and fell into dreamlessness.

PROMISES PLUS

After the morning meal, which was much like the evening meal, a call interrupted Delius's packing for the voyage ahead: *Kohav requests a meeting with the Envoy's aide Delius to discuss transcript details.*

Delius agreed to this request with raised eyebrows and said, "I don't know what that's for."

"Something to do with archives, likely," Genever said. "Though Makkow sealed them yesterday. But now we've got this far, do it whatever it is."

After a few moments Delius heard the low lisping voice call out in the atrium, "I am here, Delius!"

Delius plugged his nose with filters, socketed in a fresh oxycap, and pushed aside the heavy leather curtain that served as door: "And so am I," he said less emphatically. Kohav, tall for one of his people, was drawing himself up, doing his best to match the medium height of Delius, and the depth of his voice. "What are the transcripts that you wanted to discuss, Kohav? I thought they'd all been sealed."

"Come," Kohav said. "I will show you." And he pointed to a hallway unfamiliar to Delius, and proceeded into it, tapping with his staff and clacking in his thick leather clogs.

Delius was not eager to follow. He pushed at his mind for the right words in the language: "Please tell me where we are going, Kohav."

The Shar stopped and turned to stare at Delius. There was darkness in him, his black ungleaming eyes, sharp cheekbones, narrow mouth barely covering the tips of the fangs. His ears pointed straight up, like a devil's horns, his tail curled tensely. That was another reason for certain other civilizations not to love the Shar. They looked too much like the demons of ancient myth.

"You must trust me now, Delius. I have told one lie to bring you out here, but I will not tell another. At noon there will be a group of your people landing, but first the Emperor wants to see you alone."

The corridor ended at a walled square open to the sky and paved with worn stones, where the red sunbeams fell in dusty angles. They caught on Kohav's armlet of gold filigree. Kohav headed across to its opposite corner, and the tower that joined the two wings of the Council House. Delius followed and did not ask any more.

A few workers were moving about in the quadrangle, some laying out a morning meal for their fellows on a trestle table, others mending cracks in the walls with plaster, or running about with messages. Kohav, preoccupied, did not seem to notice them, although they noticed Delius with flashes of their black-and-red eyes and kept up conversations with whispering and hand gestures before they turned their heads away. Delius did not need to know whether they were dealing in intimacies, rivalry, or comments on the alien stranger.

At the base of the tower was an archway, the first arch Delius had seen on this world of hexagons. There were steps leading up inside it, and when they reached it Kohav lifted his free arm and gestured. "Climb."

Delius entered the cylinder of granite and climbed its stairs. A few steps up he realized that Kohav was not following, and kept going. There were lamps set into the walls, old-fashioned electric bulbs, some flickering.

The tower was tall only in comparison with the buildings around it, and after some twenty-five steps Delius found a landing whose walls were lined with instrument panels that flickered and clicked when he stepped on the floor. Detectors ... a great deal more advanced than the light bulbs. Delius was not surprised. He had visited other worlds and peoples that accepted only the technology they truly needed and no more.

Here there was another arched doorway to a room lit by lamps, and in clear and practised *lingua* Aesh Seven's voice said, "Come in."

Delius took the step. The room was high-ceilinged but small. It had two square windows. Aesh Seven was sitting on a rough wooden bench; beside him, a polished round table with grotesquely carved legs ending in clawed feet. On the table there was an oil lamp, and a heavy round stone, the emperor's seal. Aesh had no decoration but a gold clasp on the shoulder of his leather tunic.

Delius only glanced at the tableau. His sight was caught by the endless carved frieze swarming over the granite walls:

Women with babies suckling them, and children dancing, playing games, or riding the backs of their fathers. All colored in red, blue and yellow with dyes—their grains were visible—made from the soil and rocks of the land. Below these Aesh Seven seemed very dark, and radiating darkness.

Delius was forced to be aware of his own white bony face, and the white-blond hair that he combed straight back from his forehead, falling in rough shingles at the nape of his neck. Aware of those eyes, black and red, that watched.

Without greeting Aesh gestured to the walls and said, at ease in *lingua,* "These walls were created by Kessev Five. He had a grandmother." Then, "I'm sure you have noticed the detectors for sensing life and metals, but there are no devices to witness any communications into or out of this place. I want to be free to speak before your teams land. They will pretend to understand what I want of them and what I do not want. No, take notice that I don't include you among them." He gestured toward a plank bench like his own, and Delius sat.

"I try to understand."

"I realize that. I want someone to trust and I have chosen you, because you seem to be the most understanding—not because I mean any insult to the others of your party. I am taking this chance. But I must say it: if you cannot swear never to tell of this conversation I will swear that we never had it. I'm not speaking of my Council. I trust them, most of them."

Delius said nothing.

"But among aliens, you were the one who learned our language, as I learned yours. You are not afraid to look at what is left of our women, your face does not twist, and you held our child as if it had been your own." He slapped his hand on the black stone seal, with its engraved triangles and hexagons, tiny suns and planets with eccentric orbits, small embedded jewels like stars.

"I will swear," Delius said, and set his hand on the seal beside Aesh's. Even alongside Aesh's hand the coolness of the black stone drew warmth from his own as if it were blood. And again it was a case of not shivering because of the primitive depth of the ritual.

Aesh pulled back and said, "The companies that dig out our riches and bind our world in debt are quite content with its polluted state. They claim that they have made us an honest bargain, they pay us with food, because it is hard to grow on this world, with meat and leather because that is even harder to grow, with electric lights, and instruments that click and buzz. With bits of gold. They take our breath away with their smoke and filth, and we had too much of those before they came. Perhaps they believe because of our shameful history and our distaste for recording it, that we are less than intelligent."

"Not in the eyes of the Federation."

"Yes, Galactic Federation has made promises, but most of those who have tried to help us over the generations have broken themselves on this world … and we have had rumors of threat from the governors of other states, as if we had not enough trouble among our own people. Not all of our people are like me, who want to beget mothers. Some are afraid of change, some are afraid to offend our food givers, some don't want true women and are satisfied with the monsters we have. If your Federation cannot keep its promises peacefully I will not keep this tower long, and those who don't care much for Aesh Seven may like Aesh Eight even less."

"I'll work to keep those promises, but I have no power," Delius said.

"And neither do I," Aesh Seven said and drew in a breath that was his version of a sigh. "In this moment, I have this tower, and this seal," he slapped it again, "and I hope an ally among the aliens." He did not blunt the harshness of the word. "It's time for you to go, now."

Delius went past the life detectors and down the spiral stairs. Kohav was waiting at its base, but not to escort him back. He stood aside until the arch was clear, and went into it; Delius heard the cold rap of his clogs and the tapping of his staff up the steps, and crossed the square alone. The way back was straight enough.

"Now what was all that about the transcripts?" Genever was staring at him. "Makkow always takes care of them."

"I speak *lingua* better than he does." This was the truth.

A slight flush on Genever's face. "Then what was it about?"

Delius sighed. "There was some doubt about the wording, but everything seems clear enough to me."

Only too clear and a heavier burden. He hefted his baggage and went out toward coldsleep chilled already.

%⊤℣

Upstairs, in the room wreathed by the frieze of women and children, Aesh Seven nodded and gestured for Kohav to sit. "I don't want to have to trust more aliens, but these seem to want to give us something. I don't know why, but there must be a price. Their source of funds is a manufacturer of goods just as much as the ones that are working in forges and mines on our world. Of course I don't trust them completely, yet—while we have the chance I want to go ahead as quickly as possible. It will take years, but, to begin I will call a Council meeting, and … eventually I will send you out as my emissary to wherever we are called. Whatever has to be done, I doubt it will be on this world. You will choose your own aides—you know how to find the right ones."

Kohav clasped one arm with the other and looked down. "You are separating yourself from me."

"No," Aesh said quietly, almost in a whisper, "I trust you most in the world, and only the Angry-God knows what will happen to us in this country…"

Kohav had little to answer. He pulled himself up from the bench with his staff and touched the cold stone seal. The feel of it chilled him. "I'm pleased to have your trust in me." He descended the stair and crossed the quadrangle, tapping his staff and raising an open hand to clerks and officials; all replied to the gesture in varying degrees of friendship and respect. Outside the wall he walked down the dusty street while the red clouded sun rose past the quarter-mark of the day.

Presently he reached the Birthing Center, where the guards let him through the gate without question. The air was still unmoving at the open doors, and the heat as heavy inside as out. The attendants did not even turn their heads as he passed down the dark aisles of basins until he reached the one where the newborn child lay on its belly sucking the teat of its bearer. He stared down at that bearer, with its twisted knot of a head and flipper limbs.

Yes, the Emperor trusted him: he had offered Kohav's first-born son to the world.

THE WORLD SHAR:

A BROKEN HISTORY

Though there was no lack of intelligence among the Shar, their history had only one story, and that was *The Change*. All that came before had faded.

But in the beginning the world Shar hung dark and moonless under an ancient yellow star; the icecaps of its poles had devolved into shallow seas that grew unbearably hot and bitter, and its atmosphere thickened with the ash and dust of its roaring volcanoes. Even so it managed to produce a dark and stunted population of animals and the analogue of human species.

Eventually it was discovered by aliens, some of whom were Earthers. But they and all the others came only to dig in the world's soil and rock, and empty out the deep lodes of minerals, gems and fuels. The breakdown of the environment increased exponentially, and one day a Shar woman bore a limbless daughter with no intelligence and stunted senses. And another bore the same, and one more yet. The Shar, horrified, stored them away and shamed the mothers. Some mothers killed themselves after bearing these mutants.

Whatever new factor had been added to or drawn out of the

environment to cause the Change was never discovered, partly because the Shar, in their terror, did not have the means to explore it, and were ashamed to call for help. And partly because few of those who could help them knew or cared.

But in some small and isolated island nations there were groups among the population who still bred true and were suspected of some magic, or secret plotting to gain power; these were in constant danger of being overrun and slaughtered, and finally Galactic Federation took notice.

The Federation, in lean times those centuries ago, could save the true breeders only by moving as many of them as were willing to another world in the system that was cooler, but more dark and bare…

They now called themselves Meshar, meaning in their language that they had come from Shar, and most did not expect to go anywhere else but to extinction. They languished on that rock of a world, and before a standard year had passed they petitioned Galactic Federation and any other confederacies or societies they could reach, even those of possible enemies. *Settle us where life is!*

Neighboring worlds became agitated at the thought of refugee Shar swarming at their own gates, and under great pressure GalFed removed the Meshar from the desert world at huge expense and dumped them on Barrazan V, a reasonably livable world no longer used for research where the conditions were merely filthy instead of filthy and poisonous. They were happy enough, and Meshar history began here.

Generations later it was the warped and deformed society of the Shar and their dark world that called on GalFed, and it became time for the Meshar to repay the favor. Great civilizations would use their sciences and learn new skills to rectify the DNA of the Shar males, and Meshar women would be called to serve as the First Mothers of the future. No one expected them to serve willingly.

BARRAZAN V:

A DARK RESOUNDING NIGHT

Delius woke out of cold sleep on a shuttle in orbit around Barrazan V, the next stop on a very long journey. Machines armed with needles injected him with stimulants and hundreds of vaccinations, and he shivered deeply, though he had been warmed to normal temperature, and would likely be shivering at odd moments for half the next tenday. His skin was itchy from sweating against restraint pads, and he had lost the senses of smell and taste. Other machines grasped his limbs and worked them into suppleness; after that he crawled into the bath unit and let it wash him. Then, mind still cold and numb, he ate a small bland meal and fell into real sleep, he never knew how long.

Waking again with a sense of his own self now, he dressed in the crackling dark green zip that would—or might—repel dirt and water. Genever, dressed the same and smoothly combed as always, was waiting for him in the dayroom along with the archivist Makkow, now a female in estrus. Genever offered squeezers of hot tea, milk, gheng juice. Delius chose tea, though what he really wanted was vodka.

"Night will be coming on where they're going to wait for us," Genever said. "One standard day plus two hours and we board the aircar. Look down."

୬୧

One day and now night on Barrazan V, a heaping of angry rivers and sliding mountains, roaring volcanoes and jungles whipping in furious hurricanes. No one had loved the world enough to give it a name of its own, and no one thought of it without uneasiness.

The destination was wrapped in an overgrowth of the jungle, in the deserted biological station where many forms of flesh and matter had been warped to give life and death. It was part of an old story of how scientists of many worlds joined to create both new species of humanity and ever more complicated machines, until the machines awoke and overpowered the fleshly life. There were none of those left, neither the scientists nor the machines called ergs. Both learned that there was no life for them on that world, and ultimately it was given to the Meshar.

This night the Meshar clans were holding their councils, hunching in the concrete pit of the old ruined Station where both created monsters and strange indigenous life-forms had been kept, and now the cracked walls were caving in and the floor was splitting to erupt with all of the savage growth the violent world could burst on them. Outside they lived in huge leather yurts made from the hides of whatever animals they could find to skin, and carried them back and forth daily through the wild and thrashing forest looking for a calm place to pitch, so that they spent no more than two or three nights in any location.

The Meshar did not hate this world, to them it was paradise compared with Shar, where they had been hunted and beaten; if the volcanoes sent up pillars of flame and the sun shone green, it lit up a sweeter day than the ancient world that suckled their ancestors with teats forever going dry. And Meshar could breathe anywhere, with their sponge-lined nostrils.

A leader was crying out, "What will they do to us? Send us back to that lump of rock they called a moon where they dropped food and water three times a year?" There were seven or eight of their family groups crouched here, seven or eight to each group, the chosen representatives of a thin population. Some had faces that were scratched, or spotted with sores and clotted scabs, most wore scuffed leather tunics.

Here there were true women, though they did not look much different from men except for the three teats lying neatly on their chests like the points of a leather collar, two above and one below, and the tails that ended with something more like an arrow than the ace of spades.

Ladders and sliders let down Delius and Genever from the aircar to the remnants of the old landing pad along with three of their GalFed team, and a representative of Xanthrotek, ten in all, including the guards that were not visibly armed. On Barrazan V there were none of the Emperor's attendants to protect them.

Delius found the air breathable, though its heat and moisture pressed against his face like a damp pillow, with a thick smell of decaying vegetation. The storm above in the jungle's attic flung the wet green streamers of trees against each other. Lightning split the sky, and thunder crashed soon after. He hurried inside with the others.

For the use of the Meshar, parts of the station had been rebuilt, with stairways instead of the elevators that frightened them, and textured componex floors to keep their clogs from sliding. Delius and company ran down three flights and through the hatch to hear the echo of the call:

If we don't give them our women, what can *they do to us?*

And the Meshar were silent, watching the Earthers' pink and brown faces, along with a blue-skinned and a scaled one, coming down the stairs, carefully quiet and not in unison like marchers. And not all dressed in dark green. There were two women among them, but these Meshar, having women of their own, were not disturbed by strange pheromones.

There were no ceremonies or pretend celebrations here: Genever went forward first and one of the male Meshar rose to meet him Speaking in *lingua* he said, "My name is Mebarak, and you are the one named Genever, we are told. We know what you have come for. Everyone who visits here has told us of it. You want our women."

"No! That's not what we told you!" A scruffy-looking Earther with an unshaven face rose up from the floor where he had been squatting among the Meshar. He was joined by a woman who looked as scruffy, both barefoot and wearing jeans and jerseys with so many holes they looked like lace.

Delius recognized them as Vishniak and Kogol, a longtime and weatherbeaten pair of Observers who had gone native, as almost every Watcher did on Barrazan V.

Genever raised his head and said, with the slightest taint of impatience, "Then perhaps you would come here and stand with us so—"

Delius risked stopping him with a gesture; he knew better than Genever that Observers worked by standing back.

Vishniak said, "We stand for the people we're living with here, but I've told them you mean to help, and asked them to listen. Mebarak, would you listen?"

"They have come to help the Others," Mebarak said stubbornly, sounding very much like Kohav, his counterpart on the world Shar.

Delius watched the lot of them. Poor bastards, with only Vishniac and Kogol to stand between them and the universe. The Shar at least had governments, organizations, methods of supply. Here, on a world that didn't even have a name, the Meshar had only the freedom to live as men and women. What other choice?

"You were given help when you needed it," Genever said.

Mebarak cried, "Yes, and look at us now! When you want, you come running! When we need, you stay away!"

Kogol cried out, "We know how you mean to help the Shar! How will you help the Meshar?"

The representative from Xanthrotek stepped forward.

"Wait a moment," he said, "and look here!"

His name was Horrocks, and he was a tall thin man with red hair; his coverall was a white one decorated with green arabesques of ivy and leaves. Quickly on long stilt legs he stepped over the crouched Meshars carefully, and held out his hands to a child who had been grasped against his mother's side. The child cocked his head in curiosity and Horrocks gently lifted and displayed him.

"See?"

In the instant before the mother snarled and reached to grab the child back, everyone could see that his left arm ended without a hand. The end of it was not a stump, but an ending, covered with normal short fur and guardhairs.

Horrocks straightened. The faces around him looked up angrily. "I see one other of you here who is missing a hand—"

Mebarak cried out, "What are you doing to us?"

Genever said sharply, "What *do* you mean, Horrocks?"

Five or six Meshar were rising threateningly around Horrocks and he stepped away sharply. "I mean inbreeding." He tilted his head toward Vishniak. "Have you never noticed, Observer?"

Vishniak faced up to him and the Pit quieted. "I saw, and I reported," he said without anger. Then looked around for Genever and Delius. "Does anyone read—or listen to—reports in your Department?"

Mebarak broke in, "What is the inbreeding you are talking about?"

Horrocks tried to explain: "When there are only a few people to breed with, whatever fault there is in the seed—what causes sickness or crippling, goes into most of the children—"

"You mean like what happened on Shar? But they have many people—"

"But they also have many other diseases there," Horrocks said, "and a lot of filth in their air and water. If they can't get rid of that they're going to be dying faster. Where you were living on Shar it was cleaner—but you had a small group of people and there were not enough," he searched in vain for a translation in *lingua* or the local dialect for 'exogamy' "—not enough other people to mix with. You would have had no other way to find them except among other Shar."

"It was your people that brought us here!" Mebarak cried out hoarsely. "There was no other choice at all! You dropped us into this place, and yes, it is much better than the world Shar. You gave us these ones here," he gestured toward Vishniak and Kogol, "and they want to help us, not kill us as they did on Shar—but there are no supplies for them to help us with! Why should your big Federation bother with us when there are so few? There was nothing here, no buildings to live in, no tools to make them, only this place in here,"—gesturing to take in the dusty cracked floor, the writhing twists of half-withered vegetation— "where the air stinks and never moves! We carry our tents on our shoulders and run about the forest looking for places to sleep where we won't be blown into the treetops! We would build if we had what to build with and someone to teach us how. And beside all of that, all Others are afraid of us because we *shift* but we never asked the gods for that, and if it was a gift it came from the Angry-God! We live however we can! What else can we do?" He stopped, out of breath, and stood panting.

The man from Xanthrotek faced him and said, "You need more people to breed with … and there is only one place to find them."

"And they are worse off than us—that is help?"

A sharp hissing voice said, "You have forgotten the women!" At the edge of the group a woman had risen; her face was as sharp as her voice, her eyes flickered red-and-black and her guardhairs stood on end. "We came all together here to say we do not want to go to Shar and be fucked by all their men that cannot make one real woman with all the people they have! Now it is all about one that has no hand!"

Genever pushed himself forward from the background and said, "No! It is about saving worlds. Together we can make—"

"From my people you take!"

"Citizen!" Makkow stepped forward with her hands open. "How else can we save your people? And how else can we teach them to live with true women?"

To say nothing of loving them, Delius was thinking.

* * T H R E E * *

THE WORLD FTHEL IV OF THE
TWELVEWORLDS OF GALACTIC FEDERATION:

Of the twelve worlds that contain the Administrative Headquarters of
Galactic Federation, the cold fifth is where the most important business
is conducted, and the gloriously temperate number four where old diplomats go to die, or at least to retire.

A World Court rules on Fthel IV, and a large Federation adjunct, as
well as jungles that sometimes shelter outlaws, and colonies of sizes rang-
ing from village to great city. Also, there are remains of a once great civilization in huge stone arches and the giant steps that lead to them.

North of the main fork of the Serpentine River in the Great Western
Continent, attached to the clusters of Headquarters buildings, stood the
New World Hospital in privacy granted by a bay of hills covered in green
and purple foliage. A City in itself, its facilities could give care to any of
the human species on the world, and one quarter of those in Galactic
Federation. In the greatest biogenetic institute of the Federation an
extension had been built especially for the Meshar. One more among the
hundreds.

Delius's wife Natalya Beylin stood in its hexagonal chamber: a small
calm woman with olive skin and black hair. She was watching the seven

Meshar women through the one wall that was made of glass ten centimeters thick.

Outside the hexagon there were teams of scientists, researchers, more doctors, preparing instruments and watching through monitors.

But no media watched this process, by demand of the Shar and Meshar both.

The hexagon was lit by dimmed yellow lights, and visible through the glass wall was an enclosure, a round chamber, with a dim blue artificial sky, and a floor scattered with straw. The seven Meshar women had spread their mats on it, mats they had woven for themselves and brought from home, and were curled sleeping on them; the air was warmed to the temperature of their world; the atmosphere they breathed had its components, even to the molds and spores.

The Meshar breathe very softly through nostrils lined with tissue of pink sponge. While they slept it was the only tint of color on the thin black fur covering their bodies. One of them yawned and the tips of her fangs were startling white.

All seven had borne at least one child and might bear again. They were at the peak of their fertile period and tomorrow would be implanted with embryos created, like the brew of an alchemist's alembic, from their own eggs, fertilized by the modified sperm of men from Shar; after the separations of their worlds for twenty generations; ancient Shar now joining breakaway Meshar. The world would not change for this. The seven Meshar women were only a sample, but they were the emblems of a hope. Cradles.

Repeating the process in the bodies of Shar females would be another matter.

☙❧

Natalya's associate Dr. Mukherjee touched her shoulder and she startled out of her reverie. "What are you thinking, Doctor Beylin?" He was wearing the same dull blue-green cloth as her own; it was universal among Earther exomedics.

She read, or imagined, from his anxious eyebrows, that he expected her mind to be occupied with her husband, Peter Delius, sweating so often on some other mad world; and her son, James, that quiet kid, whom in spite of all their love they found so little time to care for. But she had been thinking of her father.

Natalya's father had been a doctor: *If you want to be one, on this world, don't stay with just the Earthers, there's plenty of doctors do that. You go in for exomedicine, you'll be at home wherever you are.* Not like these women.

She said slowly, "None of them chose to come here." *Like any lab animals...*

"Even if they are—eh, prisoners, it's a better place than where they were living..."

"I wonder if there ever will be an easier life for them."

Mukherjee said gravely, "No one promised them that."

He spoke in a whisper; behind them the male representatives of the Shar and the Meshar were standing against the walls in two separated groups.

Natalya had spoken with their leaders, individually; one of them was the Emperor's representative, Kohav, the first among the Shar that Delius had met; the other, the Meshar official, Mebarak, looked grim. Their silence was intense.

As a member of the team that examined the women, she had tried to communicate with them in her few words of their languages and the crabbed and primitive version of *lingua* they had managed to learn. Only one or two of them had been willing to speak at all through the microphone set into the glass; the one spoke unintelligible snarling words that could be nothing but curses, and the other, in a low hoarse voice: *You took me from my home, where there is air to breathe, and from my children…*

There were others of her clan who would care for the children, and her world was eternally lashed by storms. But.

Natalya whispered, "I'm betraying them." But no one heard.

There was a crackle, a shout, and the world blew up.

SHADOWS: RUAH

She did not know what happened or where she was, only that safety lay in darkness, because she was invisible in any shadow; and daytime shade was scarce on this world. Too much light here altogether, and sharp colors she never saw at home. The bank of leaves that had looked dark and inviting did not hide her now, and she woke sharply with closed eyes when voices began to chatter around her.

"Wot's that?"

"Some kind of animal—"

"Anybody can see that. Looks like some kind of dog you see on old screeners."

"Yeh, and they bite too."

She opened her eyes; the naked white faces of children gaped and pulled away.

"Sheez. Dogs don't have red eyes."

They did not quite speak a language she knew; it was *lingua* mixed with something else. Beyond them were green hills and trees, an area called "park." And she saw that there were metal bars closing it, with a gate. One more trap.

A thin child said in a high voice: "That's not red eyes, it has red instead of white in its eyes."

She yawned.

"And those teeth—the fangs!"

"And the tail…"

The tallest of the children, a thick one with white-yellow hair, narrowed its eyes and said, "Get a stick and give it a poke."

"Not me, you can do it!"

The thin one said, "Leave it alone, Thorny, it's not hurting you—and I bet it can really bite."

"You shut up, Deelio! I can do what I goddam want!"

Her eyes slid in their glaring reds: tolerated bully, she knew that kind well enough.

The thick one had broken off a branch and was stripping its leaves.

She stood in one flash movement and stared down at this annoyance.

The others backed away, but Thorny's eyes widened in frightened defiance, he lifted the stick and she saw the puffy white hating face in the sharp blasting sun's blue-sky light—

"Stop, Thorn, it's—"

*

A hiss of air.

"What? Where—where'd it—"

"Gone? How can—"

The animal was not there, with no sign but the hollow space it had lain in, where the pressed leaves were slowly straightening themselves.

The children stared at each other, and swallowed.

"You sure scared it away, Thorn, whatever it was."

"Shit. I'm not gonna tell anybody about this, and you lot better not either."

They suddenly felt each other's company weighed too heavy, and separated. It was dinnertime anyway. The gates opened to let them out.

*

She found herself in a squat on the thick branch of a great tree she could not get her arms around; wind and sun shook the leaves and speckled light on her. She could not tell where to go from here, but the tree was not too rough for one from such a rough world. She wrapped her limbs around its trunk and slept.

༈ ༈

The children did not tell, except one.

The smaller dining room was serving very few tonight, and certainly was a place that did not look much like home. But the child, Delius's son, who had tried to protect the stranger, was usually comfortable enough eating there with Delius, who worked at the Embassy, in the Earther Division of Galactic Federation. His mother was somewhere else; working in some hospital, he thought.

Halfway through the soup the father—a grown-up version of the child, narrow-shouldered and with a white strong-boned face—looked at the boy from under his brows and said, "Whatsit, Jimbo? You seem very thoughtful tonight." He was a quiet kid, and Delius would have liked the boy to be big and good-natured, relaxed enough to ease himself through life, instead of being a tight little knot of muscle. Too near his own introverted self. But he was the son of his mother and father. There it was.

The boy was silent for a moment, then looked up at his father, and said, "I saw something."

"You want to tell me?"

"It was a kind of animal…"

"One of those lizards that—?"

The boy muttered, "This one had hands, and reds instead of whites in its eyes, and Thorny wanted to—"

"Oh my God, Jimbo!" His father whispered harshly and flicked his eyes at the other diners, who were harmlessly staring into their soup. With effort he kept his voice down. "That was a—where did you see her?" Delius was afraid he knew what this was.

"Just inside the gate. I told Thorny he better not whack her, but she was real weird and that tail like an arrow—"

A Meshar woman, Jimbo? My God! He did not dare speak, and pushed the thought down hard for fear of telepaths. But there were none here today, and no one was wearing an impervious helmet either. "Is she still there?"

James shook his head. "No, and she had three tits!"

"Did you see where she went?"

"She just stood up and she was gone, in a kind of whoosh. I hope I don't ever see her again. She scared me. And Thorny scared me because he wanted to hit her for nothing."

Delius stood up. "This is serious, Jimbo, and I have to run. I'll pick you up at the crèche later."

He walked past the entrance of the dining room and then ran, caught the walkway and ran on that, ten steps on and his comm buzzed to tell him about destruction.

DEEPER

"What! Where are they!" The comm trembled in his hand, his voice was strangled and he did not try to clear it.

"For God's sake, Delius, stay away!" For once Genever had lost his calm. "Just stay where you are!"

"Natalya's th—"

"The chamber blew up and the whole wing is sealed! You'll never get anywhere near it!"

Delius did not take orders from Genever. "I will." He shut off and kept running down the long featureless corridors lined with easy-cleaning and colorless tile. His comm pinged and he thought: Genever pestering … and thought again. He stopped, pressed the button and listened. A woman's low heavy voice said: "You come here first."

Delius's superior occupied a cell in a glassy hive, one much like his own, but with its walls of screens glimmering in endless movement; the other clear ones looked out on offices like her own; they flickered with evening lights coming alive, workers leaving, others settling in.

Rosa Mbai was a big deep-voiced woman. Her black hair was wound into a gleaming coil at the back of her neck, and she wore a dark red tunic with a few scrawls of official embroidery on one shoulder. She had a clumsy title: Director of ExoCommunications: Hominid Division. DEX for short.

She shut down the screens as Delius came in, though her hands did not move far from the banks of keys inlaid in her desk.

"Natalya is alive," she said. "Badly injured, unconscious, they're working on her, no one can go in, it's chaos there. And the wing is closed off, we're keeping it quiet."

Delius became aware that he was sweating and panting. "Will she live! I have to see her!"

"She's alive, Delius. Genever told you, the place is sealed and—"

"The Meshar! What happened! Who—"

"Delius, we're trying to sort it out!"

"One of them got out! My son saw her two hours ago!"

"Where!"

"In the park where the children play, next to the Earther school. One of the kids threatened her and she *shifted.*"

"My God, so that's what happened when her signal went off! We'll scan—" Her fingers were on the buttons.

"Rosa, who did this?"

"We don't know for sure, and we don't know how, some explosive most likely, a suicide attack maybe, we just don't know how, possibly one of the Shar who came with the Emperor's legation."

Kohav? Surely not Kohav. "How could that happen—and why?"

"I told you I don't know, but one of those men certainly got blown to pieces, and I'm absolutely certain Mebarak would not kill the women he brought here. Not that I can't be wrong, but…"

"The women? Dead?"

"At least three of them are dead, the other three I guess barely alive. Delius, I can't let you in to see Natya, but we got Kohav and Mebarak out safely, you can guess, they're being kept apart … Kohav—one of the Shar who came with him is dead. Kohav is stunned."

Delius could imagine Kohav's agony, and Mebarak's rage. He had enough of his own. Trying not to think of all that slivered glass and Natya—

Mbai read his expression easily enough. "But Delius—you won't get inside the quarantine easily, and once you're in nobody will want to let you out."

"I know." He saw his face, twenty years older, in the reflecting glastex behind her head.

"And you know you can't say anything without being taken into custody…"

He knew that too. The reputation of the hospital. *And our sponsor, Xanthrotek.* He half-whispered, stupidly in his own eyes, "But you're out."

"I have to pretend nothing's happened."

He nodded. "I have to go collect my son," he said. "Whatever happens you can't keep me away from him."

Mbai could not make promises, and he knew that. Of her five children, three worked in various distant departments of Galactic Federation and two had traveled to Earth in search of the Africa where they wished they had been born, instead of this world of steel and polymers. She rarely saw any of them.

Delius went back down all the long corridors he had come up, and presented himself at the night desk of the crèche, where James stayed between school and dinnertime. The night-watch, a woman named Anna

Cavan, who was as motherly as she looked, said, "He's asleep, Peter, we gave him something to eat—he was so tired and … sad. Maybe you'd like to leave him with us."

He thought about that, or tried to think. His eyes were at the same time filling with tears and closing with weariness.

"You need sleep too. There's a couple of extra cots in the little room there."

He smiled thinly. "You mean the crying room. But I want to be with him when he wakes."

"I'll make sure you are."

❧❦

"Delius!"

Cavan's urgent voice.

"Yes? What?"

"I told you not to go there, you damned fool! Get up!"

That one was Genever's.

Delius pulled himself up among the spreads and curtains woven with imaginary flowers. Yesterday's memories stabbed him with horror so deeply that he had to shake the lightnings out of his eyes.

Genever stood in the main doorway, red-faced and snarling, an armed guard beside him.

"Go where? I came to be with my son."

The boy whimpered and clutched at Delius's arm. No one else but Cavan was inside the crèche and he realized that she had stayed the night to be with him and the boy.

"Gentlemen!" Anna Cavan could be something more than motherly when she chose. "You have no rights or authority here."

But Genever did not dare come in, though there was no gate or door to stop him, because of the powerful alarm system. He said harshly, "We need the boy for a witness!" He had given up his smoothness now. "We've wasted hours looking for you!"

Delius rose from the cot and put his arm around his son. "Don't bark at me, Genever." He punched Mbai's number.

"Afraid you'll have to bring the boy in, Delius," she said, sounding as if she hadn't slept, "and right away."

"I want to see Natya,"

"I'll work on it."

Delius stood up, shook down his wrinkled clothes and combed his hair with his fingers. "Thank you, Anna," he said, and took the boy's hand. "Come on, Jimbo, we're going into the cave to see…" The wizards. The monsters…

"Mother's there."

"Yes."

Parents and children were streaming down the corridor now, toward the crèche and the schoolrooms next door. Delius stood out of the way to let them pass, and James's hand tensed, but he did not pull away.

THE WORLD SHAR:

CAPITAL CITY: EQUATORIAL LANDS:

FALLING

Aesh sat alone at his table while the last light of the sun burned through the tower's window in a shaft of reddened dust. He had spent the day meeting with government committees, with the representatives of several alien industries that went through the motions of consulting him, with the committee of scientists who were preparing to give him true mothers. And after that with the secretaries who had been recording the proceedings on clay tablets as well as computers.

In earlier days he would have sent runners at this hour to bring him Kohav's child, the Father of Mothers, from the nursery where he lived with other children of his cohort. In the time that had passed since Delius left Shar for his home world, the child had learned to walk and feed himself. Aesh Seven had kept watch on him in the crèche and would bring him into the tower for a view of the world when he had a few moments free from heavy duties or weapons practice.

Now his risky choice to restore womankind to his country, if not to the world, had made his public fractious and uneasy. The decision could not be undone, and he believed in it with more passion than ever, but he was afraid to isolate the boy from his guardians.

"That's the last for today," he said to the empty air, "nothing more to do." The empty hour. He had friends, and some close ones, but none to replace Kohav, whom he had loved, but would not touch sexually—and no one with him tonight, when he felt so much at odds with himself. Servants had gone to their quarters and guards were downstairs at the arch.

He lit his lamp; an evening meal was waiting in the cooler for him to heat it, but instead he went down into the courtyard where the lamps were coming on with their blue flames, and the cooking fires had been lit. The air had cooled a little, and looking up he could see the faintest, palest glimpse of stars, like a promise of newer and fresher skies.

Workers going off duty were cooking their dinners and carrying them to the trestles; one of the guards said, "Aesh-lord, are you going to eat with us tonight?"

Aesh said, "That depends on what's being off—" and no more than that, because there was a messenger clattering toward him, panting, streaming and glistening with skin oils, his tail curved so tightly it hoicked up the edge of his tunic to one side.

"Stop!" The guard moved forward to prevent the two from colliding, but the messenger stopped on his own, gasping.

Aesh said, "What is it?"

"Terrible news," the messenger whispered.

Aesh said to the guard, "Sefer, find a cloth to dry this man." And then, "Messenger, come in and tell me!"

"No, lord, I must run back to the Hall of Communication," he gasped, and then told of the destruction on the world Fthel IV.

Aesh too found himself whispering: "Was this message sent to me, by my name?"

"For the Emperor, the message said, Aesh-lord."

The messenger seemed frightened, and Aesh said carefully, blocking his own fear and anger as well as he could, "Who sent it, tell me, who?"

"It was the being Xanthrotek."

"And what else?"

"It said: wait, until we communicate further."

"And who else received it, tell me?"

"I don't know, lord, I don't."

For one fevered moment Aesh felt the urge to make the messenger swear to keep the news secret, but did not dare.

In that instant the messenger ran away, and Aesh stood like the heaviest of stones but with a hideous shaking inside him. His claws dug into his hands and the leather of his sandals.

Sefer came back with the cloth and stared: "He's gone! What's the trouble, Aesh-lord?"

"Don't call me lord, Sefer! The Angry-God has had too much to say to me and no one will like it." He went inside the arch and took the cloth to wipe his own face and arms.

When he came out he began to hear the swelling sounds of rising voices and clacking sticks, and had a thought-flash of the angry attacker at the Birthing Center.

"I need you to come with me now. Go find my staff and bring your own."

"If you think there's a fight coming, take my staff, Aesh-lord, and I'll get another. Do we need more men?"

"No! I don't want to be seen. I want to know what's going on, and make sure Kohav's child is safe. We'll go out by the back gate and through the laneway. Keep to the shadow and don't look at anyone." They threaded their way around trash bins and over broken stones. A little rain had begin to fall, the drops burdened with the pollutants they had collected on the way down, and the lane's cobbles looked oily in the shafts of lamplight seeping in from the street.

There was a tumult roaring out of the street as they came to it, and Aesh felt a sickly fear that everyone had heard the terrible news, and knew it to be irrational. But it was real fear. He waited with Sefer at the lane's end, leaning on his staff. He heard a clacking, like that beating of sticks at the Birthing Center, when he had presented the child to the aliens and the world, and so many had cheered him; not all. And the Birthing Center was up the street just past the wall of his courtyard.

He dared look out into the lamplit street. There were groups of men beating their sticks against each other's, against walls, on the roads, some dancing and stamping and others shaking torches, some blowing hooting noises on bone flutes as if they were celebrating a holiday he had never heard of. He smelled both the torches and the toxic dirtweed the workers smoked when they were exhausted with the exasperation of taking care of all the babies, the male children, who would grow up at least, the unwomen, the cleaning, the feeding, the soothing that did very little good, all that he had so little power to ease—

And strangest, some dancers who had no sticks and no flutes had decorated their chests with pieces of leather cut into triangles, and tied around their necks with twine, that had to be imitations of women's breasts.

He took a step. "No, no, Aesh, lord!" Sefer hissed, and grabbed at his arm.

Before he could shake it away some in the rioting crowd called out, "When are we going!" And others cried, "Now! Now!"

They gave a wordless howl in unison and surged up the street as one body.

"Where are the forces?" Aesh cried, and leaped out to follow them, Sefer coming after without choice and vainly calling.

The crowd boiled down the street in a clamor of beating sticks, and the moment Aesh thought he was losing them they stopped. At the entrances of the Birthing Center and the Mother-Hall they surged about in one great swerve and the ones in front began hammering at the doors. "Get them! Get them!"

Almost completely out of breath and speechless with horror Aesh began to thrash about him with the staff which was much longer and heavier than the sticks of the rioters, and Sefer, who was younger, did the same with greater effect. By clearing away some of those around him, Aesh could see that several of the ones imitating women had managed to grab two suckling babies, and were dancing, bobbing up and down holding them high and yelling, "Here are your fathers! Here are your fathers!" Further down, out of the Mother-Hall, he saw them bearing others who were squalling with terror. Shemesh was one.

Aesh, prepared to die if need be, beat about ever more desperately, shouting, "Stop!" not even believing he could be heard. He took hold of his staff by its heavy end, raised it above his head and slammed it down on the paving stones. It shattered with a wrenching noise that was like a shriek. A few around him scattered at the sound, Aesh found himself with Sefer in a small open space, and ran across it to grab the child Shemesh from the rioter's arms.

At that moment alarm bells rang, helmeted guards pushed out of the Center's doorways and surrounded those who had grabbed the babies. These were being plucked away by nurses. Six more guards appeared aiming crossbows, weapons that Aesh himself had earlier ordered them to bear, for protection of the children.

Some of the rioters were scared into *shifting,* the rest of the crowd dropped their burned-down torches and faded. By now the lamplight had picked out the glint of Aesh's gold clasp, there was a whisper of *Emperor* from the rest of those who had separated from their crowd mind and become only tired and embittered people recognizing their Emperor, like him or not.

Aesh said to the guards, "Put your weapons away. I will take care of the child." Shemesh quieted down but trembled in Aesh's arms while Aesh caught his breath.

Sefer offered his staff and Aesh settled the child on his hip and took it with his free hand. "Not home yet," he said. He could see protest in the tenseness of Sefer's mouth. He went on up the street, leaning more heavily on the staff now, to the Mother-Hall, a large cubic building of ochre brick, with an ironic name for a place where motherless children lived. There was a guard here now, with a crossbow in hand too late to be of use. The lights in the doorway let him recognize Aesh.

"You are free to come in, or I will take the child, lord," the guard said.

"No. I want to speak with the minder who cares for the child Shemesh," Aesh said. The guard absorbed this and opened the doors for him, but kept back Sefer. Aesh left Sefer with his staff and went in. He waited in the vestibule and waged a hard battle with sorrow and fear.

Presently a young man came past the shutters that closed off the inner room. He was wearing the usual uniform of green synthetic fibers, another incongruous technological marvel of his world. Aesh had met him several times when he was on daytime duty, and trusted him.

"You asked to see me, Aesh-lord."

Aesh, too weary to be anything but blunt, said, "I'm sure you know of what happened out in the street this night."

"Our guards have just told all of us here."

"I and my guard fought our way through those ones. This child was in grave danger in the hands of rioters and I took him." He spoke in a tone of voice that was far from boasting.

"Eh, have you been hurt?"

"No, but I am afraid for Kohav's child, and I want to take him with me to a safe place away from this district, that those angry people don't know. He will be well guarded … ask your supervisor."

The minder looked hard at him. He would be obliged to do what the Emperor asked, but he would not do it easily. He said slowly, "You wish to become responsible for him."

Aesh thought of *the destruction* and *Here are your fathers!* and barely repressed a shudder. "I will be responsible," he said.

༄ ༺

When Aesh came back out with the wrapped and sleeping child still riding his hip and a borrowed staff in his other hand, Sefer gaped at him. "Bear with me, Sefer," Aesh said. "We still have a distance to go."

"I'll help you," Sefer held out his hand for the child.

"No, let me carry him, no one will stop me." And Sefer thought he looked still fierce enough with his staff pounding the stones and his arm around the child.

Aesh then laid down a zigzag course of lanes and alleys, with sudden turns and narrow byways. "This is the short way," he said dryly. The sky had thickened, and there were few lamps alight; though red fireflies swirled around him like sparks from the torches far behind him, they gave no light to the way ahead. There was an occasional scratch of lightning followed by barely audible thunder; raindrops came down once in a while with their burdens of soot, but Aesh was surefooted.

"No one is following," Sefer said. Nothing else was alive in the alleys, except for the fireflies and a few unseen rat-like animals skittering and gnawing.

"I know," Aesh said. "Now down this way."

At the same moment they stepped out of the lane into a street. It was a blind street, crescent-shaped and set into a shallow basin of land, its flank rising in a vast and jagged landscape of broken walls, the ruins of great structures built in times beyond memory. Now they were shattered and ragged walls of plastered stone, too broken to rebuild and too extensive to clear away with the equipment available locally. Where the land levelled off on the other side of the street, there were several clusters of small stucco houses that somehow fitted with their ancient surroundings.

Aesh lengthened his stride and went straight to the street's end, to the last house, a three-roomed building with yard enough for a coal-pot and a cooking spit, and thumped on the door with the staff.

"Wake up, Ohr-father! Your son Aesh needs you!"

The words aptly summarized the relationship between Aesh and his father.

After some mutterings, curses perhaps, with rattling and scraping within the house, the door opened and someone peered at him out of the darkness.

"Is that really Aesh-lord?" Aesh recognized the voice of his father's guard.

"Only Aesh, Har. Is my father too deeply asleep to—"

"I am very well awakened," another voice said. "Don't wake everyone else around us." A deeper voice.

"I was afraid that I wouldn't find you." Aesh was weak with relief, but did not dare give in.

"Why have you come?" Ohr stood in the doorway. He was twenty years older than Aesh and did not look that; he was not so tall, but when the two were together it was subtly apparent that he had the more powerful personality; Aesh as a child had felt that his father's eyes gave off light. Ohr had been an influential City Councillor, and was now retired with the house and caretaker/guard that were his reward.

"What is that you have in your arms?" They had not seen each other for nearly a year, and Aesh found no change in his father.

Aesh took breath. "Kohav's child."

"Are you mad? The Angry-God will eat you for that!"

"I took him away to keep him safe. I want you to keep him for me, I arranged it with the Mother-Hall. And also let me in out of the rain."

"You *are* crazy!"

"Are you going to send me away?"

"Come inside! You are frightening me."

"Not as badly as I've been frightened." He said to Sefer, "Come in with me and sit down."

"I will sit down out here," Sefer said. "I am a guard, not a guest." He squatted on the doorstep.

"You have a loyal servant," Ohr said.

"I need him."

Inside, Har had lit an oil lamp, and had gone off to find a mat for the child to sleep on. In the main room there was a table, two benches and a stool; aside from the lack of technological devices, very much like Aesh's room in the tower. The kitchen had a sink with a water-pump, and a small root-cellar beneath. The walls were of the same pale stucco as the exterior and decorated with nothing but a set of shelves.

Ohr motioned Aesh to one of the benches and sat on the other. Aesh set the child on the mat; Shemesh was well built and very active by day, and always earned a hearty sleep. He did not even whimper.

"And what am I to do with him?"

"What you did with me when you served your term in the Mother-Halls. He will eat whatever you do," Aesh said. "Tell everyone it is your grandson from the north country."

"You should not have said that, Aesh."

"You are right. I should not."

"How do you expect to keep this secret?"

"You've always said you didn't care to be known as the Emperor's father, and no one does know."

Ohr admitted to that, and added, "You look very tired. You may sleep here if you need to."

"No! Everyone would find that very suspicious."

"Then tell me why you have brought the child."

"I was walking out and I found the disturbance in the street…" Aesh told the rest of the story.

They spoke in the old tongue they had both grown up with in the northern part of the country where they were born. They had been forced to leave because of the volcanic eruptions that intensified pollution of an atmosphere that was already foul.

Ohr said, "You still have not explained why it was so urgent."

"The rioters in the street would have killed him. They were holding him above their heads and screaming."

Ohr was silent for a moment. "Did you never know of this kind of disturbance before now?"

"No … I never did. I didn't realize that I was so ignorant. Or perhaps I wasn't watching and listening closely enough. But you knew?"

"I knew of some, though not as extreme as this one. I walk in the streets more than you do, Emperor."

"I am not a Civil Leader of this city. But if you want to take my seal of office you have only to pick it up. I find it heavy enough and perhaps you would carry it better."

"That was not meant as a slur. Only an observation. But you have not been watching carefully enough, Aesh! Eh, bad luck that you are sterile, Aesh-seed. If you had had children you would have known much more of what is going on in the crèches."

Aesh forced himself not to hang his head like a child. He had three mutant sisters, and he was Ohr's only son. "I served my own time in those places for long enough, and with those—the unwomen, as well, and when I was serving there nothing like this went on. No, that is not quite true—but it was rare."

"Now there are more aliens and even filthier air. You have made great promises and … people are angrier…"

"That I know, and it's one reason why I've brought you this child."

"This is a terrible risk you are taking, Aesh. For both of us."

"Yes. Greater than the risks you took to beget one son. And all I have worked for may fail. And all those in the streets may tear me in pieces. But let us say for now that I am bringing you a child."

"I will hire another guard."

"I would send you one of mine, but—"

"No! That would be foolish. I still have a few connections." Ohr picked Shemesh up off the mat as if he was made of air; he stirred and squalled a little, but settled in the crook of Ohr's arm. "Until you come to reclaim him he will be one of my own."

Aesh left him then, and went home with Sefer in too-quiet city streets.

੭੨੮

In the courtyard there was only the accustomed quiet now.

"You've served me bravely, and I will repay," Aesh said. "Go and eat. I want to walk by myself for a while." He was limping with tiredness and Sefer watched him. Near the arch a doorway in the wall opened into a small chapel, and Aesh went inside. It was a dark stone-lined place with a high ceiling that had no decoration and represented nothing; there was an altar where once in ancient times some sacrifice might have been made that was made no longer and the floor was littered with the broken idols of forgotten gods. No one worshipped there; but sometimes people came to placate the Angry-God with a small gift, a piece of fruit or wreath of dried grass, a marbled stone or some strange insect with a luminescent shell.

These are sterile things, like myself. Aesh knew too well that his shame over his sterility had closed his inner self to others, no matter how greatly he cared for them, and kept him from offering intercourse to anyone, male or female.

Sefer, still on watch, called to several acquaintances to bring him food from the trestles while he stood duty. When he had finished eating, he realized that Aesh had not come out of the chapel, and went there to find him. The emperor was crouched on the floor with his arms clasping the altar, and deeply asleep. Sefer woke him, carefully, and did not tell anyone.

* * F O U R * *

ETHEL IV:

R U A H

Waking up with her arms around the tree. There she was, in darkness, bits of bark in her fur, guardhairs bent, skin itching from the contact. It was quiet here, no children to torment her—and none to love, either—and she climbed down, wanting a drink of water. Not worried about food, yet. Shar and Meshar both knew a great deal about going hungry, and their metabolisms had accommodated.

But alone.

My children have other mothers and my men have other women to fuck. So then...

Where am I? And what? I am I and this is here. Out of that smash/ blood/howling place. Where to, then? Home is a different world. All of that stupid talk of old know-it-alls: *There are three worlds, Ruah my daughter! One you live in, one you go to: that broken-off half of a people that is your new world, and one you stop in on the way.*

Here is the one I stop in on the way, and nobody to say what next.

She climbed down to find out.

There were many more trees around her, not wild things with ever-breaking branches like at home, but great pillars she could not get her arms around at their bases; they had huge sweet-smelling leaves that the wind could barely ruffle. She moved out from under them into a small clearing, staring around to find a direction—

And a hoarse voice cried out, "What's this thing here?"

Two beings dressed in rags—Earthers?—stepping off a tramped-down path between trees. Speaking a rough *lingua* she could barely grasp.

"I dunno, I never seen anything like it."

Coming closer as she pulled back. They stank, even to a nose as tolerant as a Meshar's, of filth and fermented matter. Wanderers, beggars maybe, she knew some on her world, who tramped from clan to clan on a bad season whimpering for food—and were given it if there was any to spare. But she did not know what these ones would want from her.

"Looks like, eh, some kind of dog? Wolf? Like they used to have on Earth—"

"Well, if it looks like food let's kill it."

Not much to see of them in the starlight, but the morning light was coming up … and these words she understood.

These were not children. "I am not your food and," her voice deepened, "I am not your dog."

They had dark red faces that were shrunken as if their sun had burned them down. Perhaps many suns on many worlds. "Well maybe there's something else we can do with you, don't you think, Mert?" the taller one said, and reached down into the sack hanging from his shoulder.

Before she was sure he had a knife, before he could quite get it out, she was on him with all her claws digging, fangs bared and tail thrashing. He fell back whimpering. She squatted astride him, grabbed the knife from his pocket, touched the point edge up to his neck and growled in her own language, "Yes, something else to do?"

The one that he had called "Mert" did not try to rescue him but screamed and ran.

She pulled away. "Get up." He hitched himself up and ran after, yelling, probably cursing his faithless friend.

She howled after them, "Some world this is with people like you in it!" But they were far away and anyway did not understand her language. She pushed the knife into the ground and stamped down the handle so it drove deep to rust in the soil.

Cry it out, cry it out, Ruah! They will all think you are some beast and run to close you in walls like the others, what is left of them!

These had been weak evil ones. She was very sure there were many stronger. And though she had not drawn blood, and only gotten some of their dirt on her—she spat—she was disturbed with herself for being angry instead of merely frightened, and *shifting*. What she had felt with her red-veined claws stretching and her lips drawn back to bare her fangs was a strange sense, almost of pleasure, from a savage and ancient past. On another world, not this one.

Meshar were variously proud, sensitive, sometimes short-tempered, and particularly, sardonic. But there were too few on the home world for battles and blood-fights. What was the use of war when the enemy kept disappearing?

Really thirsty now. On the pathway in the before-morning stillness she could just hear water purling thinly over stones.

Water to drink first, and then find food.

〷〵

DEPTHS

His home world had become unreal to Delius as he was ferried deep in the tunnels down the long moving walkways between Headquarters and Hospital, with the overhead lightstrip flaring to yellow-green fluorescence overhead as he passed, James gripping him with one hand and the other touching the railing; both silent and thinking almost the same thoughts they did not need or want to share. The walkway creaked and ticked with some minor dysfunction, and branched off into a half-score of elsewheres dictated by luminous arrows, and stretching on forever.

∿∾

When he was going anywhere along on a walkway, moving or not, Delius always ran. There was no place for exercise in the old and shabby Terrarium. The grand and beautiful marble halls with crystal ceilings were meant to impress new peoples from newfound worlds, and trod on with stately steps.

He would not run here now, holding James's trusting hand, and his slow steps were agony.

NATALYA

Opening her eyes, slits of light into strangeness. Everything white around her. Where?

Delius looking down at her. And the boy beside him.

Oh. It's all right, then, isn't it?

No. She opened her eyes again and whispered faintly, "Couldn't help them—"

The whiteness of it all. Pressing on her.

"We know, dear."

A reedy voice crying *Mother* and asleep again.

She was enclosed in a force-field and he could not have touched her if he dared.

∿∾

After that the ride back was too short for Delius's need to stay with her, and he was only barely conscious of his son's hand tightening in his, and then they were shunted into a cell with Mbai in her crystal hive.

Workers moved around them in the glassy walls beyond. There was no sign of Genever. Delius knew that Genever was expecting to move up to Mbai's position; perhaps the distance was greater than he had believed.

"This part will go quickly," Mbai said. She drew a breath and said quietly, "James, I've been told that you saw something unusual yesterday."

"Yes."

"Please tell us about it."

"I was with some kids and…"

And on, nervously, through the painful recitation.

"And who wanted to poke her with a stick?"

"I can't tell you that. I wasn't supposed to tell anything. He'll think I told just to get him in trouble, and he'd beat me up and the others are my friends."

"We'll find a way to protect you no matter what. But," she turned to the Delius, "what about those other children?"

Delius said, "Eventually everyone will know, and all we can do is delay that. Right now you still don't know any more than you knew yesterday. I don't want to see my son put in a box where he has no mother and no friends and his father sent off God knows where. And I don't think you want any of the media getting a hint and going after the kids for the news. If you want to make it safe for him, put guards in the school and the crèche, call them Superintendents, that'll keep everybody safe and put a stop to any bully."

"I'm for it," Mbai said. "Guards are a good idea. I'll call someone to take your son back, Delius. Do you feel safe enough to go back to the crèche if we send in a guard, James?"

"Yes ma'am, if he keeps, um, that one from jumping me."

"She will."

The guard came to collect James, and they watched the boy being led through the maze of windows. Then Rosa Mbai said, "We had to do that, search in all directions, even if we didn't learn anything new. But this next part may not go so quickly."

"What are you saying?"

"Genever has made a statement in which he claims that when you and he were on the team negotiating the agreement with the Shar—"

"All the way back there?"

"—that you and Kohav went off to have a discussion you claimed was about checking the accuracy of Makkow's transcripts of the meetings, both yours and those that were left with the Shar—"

Delius began to sweat. "And?"

"—but that later on, when you were back here and he handed them in, they had their original seals and dates and obviously had not been opened or changed."

"And he never mentioned this before." Delius felt suddenly naked in his wrinkled clothing and finger-combed hair, his feelings burning on his face.

"He claimed it hadn't occurred to him until now. I don't know for God's sake, Delius, I never hired Genever but I have to work with him. He's made this accusation and I have to investigate it. Tell me you and Kohav were talking about those transcripts, or whatever you really were talking about."

All I need say: I swore an oath to the Emperor: see what happens then. James had said, I can't tell you who the bully was. Natalya's breath was so frail, he wanted only to stay and watch her breathe.

"What's important about connecting me with Kohav?"

"Because it's possible that somebody outside that chamber did something to help someone inside blow it up."

The anger rode over the fear then: "My God, I've worked with you all these years, do you really believe that of me!"

Wrinkles that he had never noticed before broke out in her face. "No, Delius, but you spoke with him privately, you told a lie then about those damned transcripts … don't you think I've been up all night in meetings with all the doctors and researchers trying to understand this horrible tragedy? Delius? You made some kind of private deal…"

"I spoke with him, all I did was, I swore to do my best to see that they were treated honestly, I didn't make promises for anybody else to keep."

"But without our authority and permission. I can't let that go."

He managed to stop himself from saying, *What deal's Genever going to get for telling you all this?* But he said bitterly, "Genever's been saving this up for a while."

"He won't get much credit for it. It's something I really didn't want to know. I'm not taking any action now, you're not going to run away from Natya and the kid. You'll be called up for it, but not now." She added, in a half-smothered voice: "You must have guessed by now, Genever has some connections with Xanthrotek."

Delius took a deep breath and said, "Just keep him away from me."

Mbai's voice tightened. "Are you making threats, Delius?"

"Only that I might spit in his face."

THE PROJECT

Delius went back to his quarters to wash and change his clothes. Fresh clothing gave him a temporary shell, and he did not care whether he came late to the next meeting of scapegoat-seekers.

On his way down the residence hall toward the meeting room, about to enter the tunnels, he noticed that the last doorway to his left was half-open and someone was—not leaning but slumped against the frame, head down. He could not tell who, at first, because of the light from the room beyond, and then realized that it was Horrocks, the tall one, the supervisor from Xanthrotek … the sliding door moved slightly back and forward, gently nudging him to make up his mind, go in or out.

Delius paused. He liked Horrocks, and believed him to be honest and competent; he had not seen him since their return. The man had every right to be present at the culmination of the project he had been guiding; now he looked as if its destruction had collapsed him as well.

He was very pale, beyond the usual pallor of the redhead, with a bright spot of flush on each cheekbone, looking even hotter contrasted with the sludge-colored cloth of the uniforms favored by the department. His eyelids were red and swollen.

Delius could barely think beyond his own misery, but forced himself to say, "Are you all right, Horrocks?"

Horrocks turned his head, with great effort, and said, "What do you think?"

Delius said, a bit sharply, "I thought you might be ill, and need help."

Horrocks shook his head. "I'm sorry, I didn't mean to snap like that. I stayed at the hospital all night … three of them are dead, and one other may not survive … I don't know why, or how … my God, who could have wanted to do … I was sitting there with them … and—and I loved those women. Really loved them. I don't mean I wanted to fuck them or anything like that…"

Delius wondered if Horrocks was younger than he looked, but no, he was simply exhausted, trying to pull his mind away from the horror.

"I knew what you meant."

"I don't think you quite understood—I got to know them, the way those old natives Kogol and Vishniak on Barrazan Five knew them. And the one that's gone missing, Ruah, you remember how she spoke up when we met them on Barrazan Five, the sharp one … you see, the project was mine."

"Yours?"

Horrocks stumbled over his tongue for a moment. "Um, my name isn't really Horrocks…"

Delius found himself gaping again. "It's not—?"

"I mean—that's my mother's name. My own name is Derek Vanbrennan."

It rang in Delius's mind. "Xanthrotek…"

"Yes. That was my grandfather who founded the company. My father was the CEO, he's about to retire and—is there something wrong with that?"

"It's the surprise. I'm just trying to fit the name to you."

"My father wanted me to join the firm because he thought I'd do well, I'd had medical training and I was a supervisor—you don't need to know all this."

"I want to know. You used to work alongside my wife, and she was never allowed to tell. Now we're both inside the walls here, you can tell."

"Well I was a supervisor in our branch on Fthel V, where it's always raining, and I worked hard and kept my name off the rolls so nobody could call me Daddy's boy. Then my father wanted me here, and I came. I did well," his voice caught and he swallowed, "I was head of the team that lifted the Österkhan off Oerstmann Six and settled them on Pembo Four. They were a bad-tempered bunch and I was glad to be shut of them, but they haven't complained—and we won a Federation Award for that and … then of course I had some part in discovering why all those Shar females—women … deteriorated … this Shar project depended on me—I'd rather kill myself than have my father…"

Delius found himself crying out, "Oh, no you wouldn't, Horrocks, no you wouldn't! You're just finding out what goes with the territory, that will get patched up somehow and you'll move on. Don't slump there dying in the doorway, get some sleep, and I'll report whatever hellish business is going on over there, for you. God damn it Horrocks, my life is tied up in this too!"

"I know that. I didn't mean to make it any worse for you."

"You haven't. If it gets worse for me it'll only be because whatever I've done wasn't good enough." *And Aesh-lord, I did my best for you, you poor bastard, but you'll die without ever knowing that … and it doesn't matter now.*

＊ ＊ F I V E ＊ ＊

THE WORLD SHAR;

CAPITAL CITY EQUATORIAL LANDS

Aesh Seven woke from a dream in which the not-women rose from their endless sleep and began to speak terrible words. He crouched once again alone in his tower. His new bodyguard, Sefer, stood below at the entrance, waiting to stop all those that would do away with the Emperor: one against how many? Was Sefer really faithful? Would the population of the world really rather keep casting their seed into the brainless lumps lying twitching in tubs and baskets, spending endless hours forcing food down those gullets, cleaning up that endless piss and shit—than contend with all the complications of relationships with a truly female sex? Perhaps the women in those friezes around the walls were jeering at him for his arrogance.

Aesh asked himself all number of questions but had no answers for them, and gave up, pulling himself from his bedding with backflashes of nightmare. The chief cook stationed in the courtyard brought him his breakfast of slivered meat and sliced root vegetables. Sefer had wanted to taste it for him, but he refused. "I am not quite a coward yet, Sefer, but if you taste my food for me I will look like one. It is enough that I never felt I needed a bodyguard until you gave yourself to the service." Then he had asked without giving himself time to think, "Would you rather not have women on this world, Sefer?"

"Aesh-lord, my father gave half his life feeding and cleaning my womb-bearer."

A vote from one, who sat on nobody's Council and had no vote.

And again, questions. The message he had received about the destruction of the most important experiment in the world, was identified only with the name Xanthrotek, with no suggestion of anyone else receiving it … was it really true?

It was no surprise at all on this morning that a messenger would come to the foot of the stairwell and call up with deep echoes to tell him that he was wanted at the Council table.

"By whom?"

"Your Council and the being Xanthrotek."

"When I am ready," Aesh called down, swallowing on his apprehension.

Another voice called, "I will come up!"

Aesh recognized the voice: leader of the Council Guard, an official appointed by his predecessor. This guard answered to the Council.

"No you will not," Sefer cried

"Who are you to speak to me like that?"

"I'm his guard!"

"Needs a bodyguard now, does he? Hiding something? You stand aside, I can bring plenty here to make you!"

Aesh leaned out of the window. "You, Chief of Guards! Before the sun reaches noon you will be digging in the death-fields, you shut your mouth and wait!"

He went back and crouched in his basin, squeezing a soaking cloth over his head, stood to let it run off, and poured the basin-full into a drain to be tanked and filtered. No way to drain and filter his fate.

The guard yelled, "Where is the child?"

Aesh did not answer. He wrung the cloth over the grating so that it would catch the last drops.

But the guard rattled his staff against the doorpost. "You must come with me," he growled, "the Council is sitting now!"

Aesh pulled his tunic over his wet fur, found his clogs and set his feet into them, let the breath drain out of him and raised his eyes to look around once at the frieze on the wall as if he might never see it again. An exaggerated idea, but he felt so, going down the staircase with its flickering lights.

Sefer had found a new staff for him, and he crossed the diagonal of the courtyard toward the Council House among the servants and messengers who had been clearing up after breakfast, and were glowering at the Chief of Guards.

The walk across took only a few moments but Aesh found it long enough in the heat among the bars of the sun's rays angled in dust.

As he was about to step over the threshold he heard a babble of voices in the street, and one beyond the wall crying out, "Angry-God destroyed Woman because she was foul and evil!"

He felt hot and cold at once. *What use?*

THE COUNCIL

The Council room's square walls were the same ochre brick as the outer ones, and a circle of stone pillars held up the roof. The thirty-nine Councillors and four outworlders sat around the hexagonal table of some deeply burled and alien red wood.

Aesh found it hard going to look at the lot of them with a bold face, and he knew that the Council members read this in him. Nevertheless he said, "Will the Archivist take note that this Council meeting was not called by the Emperor?"

"Noted," the Archivist said.

Aesh saw that his usual bench at the table was free for him to take it;

the outworlders were four representatives of alien industries here, a Bimanda, a Varvani and two Earthers, all of whom he knew well from earlier discussions.

He sat down on his bench as if it were for the first time.

Next to him, his Prime Minister twisted round to face Aesh, saying, "You were seen last night down in the Road of Halls carrying away the child you call Father of Mothers." This was a man named Givor, who had come second in the voting for Emperor. Givor was no enemy, but not quite a friend either.

Aesh said, "Only by rioters in the streets! Whoever saw me should have come to help me! I was frightened for him! Rioters had pulled him and other children from the Mother-Hall and the Birthing Center and were threatening to drop them! What would you have done? Put extra locks on your gates and gone to sleep?" He added, "And the child *I* call Father of Mothers? If you didn't agree with those plans you had only to say so."

"Plans are one thing and carrying them out another. What have you done with the child?"

"I have put him in a safe place."

"Where?"

All those eyes, intent.

"I will tell you if all but the Councillors leave."

Givor growled an order. And said, "Now."

Aesh had no talent for lying. "I gave him to my father. He was once a Civic Authority and everyone trusts him as I do."

"Where does he live?"

"You must promise not to charge him with mischief!"

"We do! Now where?"

"In the last house on the road by the Great Ruins."

Givor said, "The child must be returned, Aesh, and we will give him more guardians if you feel it necessary." And added, "But now we also have the terrible news that the place on the Galactic Federation world that was caring for the women from Meshar has been destroyed."

"Who told you of that news?"

"The Communications messenger, and I told all the rest. Is there something wrong in what I did?"

"I only wondered why we were told separately, and if there was someone who wanted to stir disagreement among us." *And would have done so very well if I had tried to keep that news secret.*

"Whoever it was, or what it means—what shall we do with the plans now? And especially when you endangered this child that everyone knew of by taking him from the place where he was cared for, in all that stir of people for everyone to see!"

Aesh bowed his head. "When I heard of that destruction I went half mad from sorrow and anger for a while, and then when I saw what was happening in the streets with very few trying to stop it, I thought it might be that almost everyone was against all those plans and not as I had believed … they were dancing and screaming, mocking even the prospect of women, and seizing children from the nurseries, and I was afraid those rioters would kill him … and I tell you, the guards were far away."

"The guards who drove the rioters away tell us that the Mother-Halls were not being attacked," Givor said. "I find it hard to believe that the child was in real danger last night."

"He was grasped and held up by the hands of a screaming rioter! If your witness denies this he must be blind!"

"That's as may be." Givor gestured at the Councillors. "We've discussed this, and we all agree that you must return him, no matter what happens with our plans." Then he looked at Aesh sharply and said an odd thing. "Tell me, Aesh, do you consider this child yours?"

Givor had sons. Aesh said passionately, "I wish that he was. I know I must return him, and admit that I made an error, but I was afraid for him—and I will step down from that tower if everyone votes on it."

Perhaps that Seal is too heavy a stone for me. And the child too heavy for me to carry.

A urgent voice cried, "Wait!" The speaker was an Earther named Dos Ramos, who sat in Council and worked for Xanthrotek in the orbiting offices.

"We made our agreements with your emperor Aesh Seven. He has always been honest with us, and most of us agree with cleaning the atmosphere and restoring the mothers. If you make him go you will look vulnerable to the Polar Territories at both poles. We must see what we can save here, and rework our plans."

It seemed clear enough to Aesh that the aliens were unwilling to interrupt the mining of precious metals, gems and liquid fuels with the election of a new Emperor. But he pulled himself away from the thought, because bitterness lay there. *And any child will do as a father if we ever have hope of finding a mother.*

The Council had no more to say, except for Givor's last word. "I will give you an escort to bring the child back." And, looking around at all Councillors: "We cannot keep this news secret forever, but we need not spread it about either."

BLOOD

Aesh, returned to his tower, waited for the escort. He dared not look at the frieze of women and their children, but did his best to turn his mind away and sat watching as the sun climbed through barely translucent clouds to the peak of the sky. The clouds thickened and rain began to fall in splattering drops. Unexpectedly he began to feel hungry, and went down into the wet courtyard to eat a meal once more with the workers who had unfolded hemp awnings over the trestle tables.

As he was finishing it he heard the purposive steps behind him, and a voice said, "We are ready. Will you come?"

He turned and was surprised to find Dos Ramos, armed with a stunner, along with the Chief of the Guards. Painful as his feelings were, he was pleased. In his edgy dealings with aliens, Aesh had always gotten on well with Dos Ramos; partly because like Delius he was fairly fluent in the language, and perhaps also because with his short stature, thick black head of hair and beard, and bristled limbs, Dos Ramos looked as near as an Earther could to a Shar. And was probably, Aesh thought, chosen for this reason.

Aesh nodded at him and then said, "Sefer, you will come with us as well."

Having fortified himself against the Chief of Guards, he led the way out of the courtyard, back the way he had gone, in much the same rain. Past dripping men lugging trash bins, through the back gate and over slippery stones down the lane where other men were pulling wheeled and creaking carts filled with coals, firewood, hairy-rooted vegetables or sterile-packed food and drugs supplied by outworld ships. The four did not speak as they went, and did not need to.

Under the heavy sky the streets were not much brighter than the night Aesh had traveled through, and a few lamps had been lit. The Birthing Center was shut tight with guards at its entrances, but the storehouse, which had been only a dark and massive great cube the night before, stood open now; carts and rattling wagons heaped with animal hides and sacks of grain and vegetables were being pulled in and out of its doors by lumbering bossuks, a species of cattle engineered on a distant world for meat and labor on Shar and other places with extreme conditions. The Chief of Guards bullied his way through all of these, knocking against them with his shoulders, tapping them with his staff.

Beyond the storehouse and on the other side of the road was an array of markets hung with festoons of lanterns where wagons were being unloaded and merchants arranging trays of foods, water-pitchers, knives, cleansers, axes; buyers picked at them and dealt out bits of unmarked metal shaped like triangles, circles, pentagons in exchange.

Children too old for the Mother-Halls, and too young to begin their life's labors, were everywhere among their fathers' limbs, yelping and splashing in puddles careless of the steady rain, poking at each other, pulling each other's tails or holding onto their fathers'. Careful not to pull those! Aesh, who had lived this life, watched them intently and without nostalgia as he walked: where last night's rage had been the worst of this city, this dim-lighted day was the best it could provide.

None of the workers here looked at Aesh or his escorts, and Aesh thought they were turning their eyes away. Their only sign of recognition was by one mischievous child who grabbed the Chief Guard's tail and gave it a hearty yank, and Sefer, good watchman that he was, blocked the retaliatory slash of the Guard's staff.

Beyond this market was the Central Mother-Hall. Around this great vault of a building there was a courtyard of hard-packed dirt where younger children scratched circles and ladders for their jumping games, but it was empty today, with everyone inside. Aesh could not help thinking of other halls deeper into desolate places inland where there were no children at all, but only basins of aged unwomen slowly dying, and more than likely—inevitably—some helped along by their weary keepers.

Past that place Aesh did not take the dodging roundabout way to his father's house when he had thought he was traveling in secret, but quickened his step down the streets of small houses and triangular huts where believers worshipped Angry-God, and few were on the streets on a working day. Aesh found himself breathing hard now, almost running toward the road by the Great Ruins where he had left the child. There was one crackle of thunder, then the rainfall drifted away and the sky began to lighten.

Around the last corner—"What's that!"—Dos Ramos cried out and ran ahead. At the end of the gravel road Aesh could see a flurry of figures and sticks thrashing, punctuated by yelps of pain.

After that there was stillness; three or four curious people crept from their houses but Aesh was struck by a lightning-shock of fear and began to run. He could see his father's old guard Har, half-stooped and leaning on his staff, blood streaming down his jaw to his shoulders, and Dos Ramos going up to the old man to support him, but there was no sign of his father or the child. He ran, pounding at the gravel road with the butt of his staff, half jumping—

Someone was lying still at Har's feet. Aesh stopped there and found himself staring down.

By its skewed angle he could see that the attacker's neck was broken; the body was bruised and bloody but the face was clear, and Aesh recognized the messenger from the Hall of Communication who had brought him the news of destruction. One hand still held a staff, and the other an axe. No one else in sight.

The Chief of Guards shooed away the murmuring watchers but Aesh hardly noticed. "Where's my father, Har? Where is he!" Beyond control his voice became a hoarse scream.

The old man twisted to look at him but was too far gone with pain and weariness to speak. Dos Ramos said quietly, "Most likely he *shifted,* lord."

"No, no! Not with that child!" He ran into the house and could see no one. Sefer ran after, crying out, "Aesh-lord, there may be more than this one!" but he ignored the call and frantically searched corners and shadows, hardly able to breathe.

"Stay back, Sefer!" A table, two benches, nothing. He made himself stand still, to think, think hard, heard the sound, a mewling, a small animal's cry. He ran into the kitchen and under the sink, among the root vegetables and beside the coal basket, he found Ohr crammed in, eyes closed and limbs folded, and trapped in back of him the whimpering child. Aesh howled, "Ohr-father!" and Ohr opened his eyes.

"Ah-ya," he whispered, "everything has fallen apart, Aesh-seed."

But a moment later Aesh was squatting on the stone floor with

Kohav's filth-covered son in his arms.

"Not everything, Ohr-father. Not everything."

❧❧

Dos Ramos used his comm to summon an aircar that would deliver Har to the medical facility in the nearest mining station. The old man would need some mending but his wounds were already clotting: evolution had given the Shar more gifts than *shifting*.

Sefer had found a few rags and was boiling water over the coal-pot to wash Ohr and his charge, who were more dirty than damaged. The Chief of Guards was squatting on a bench, looking out the window into the distance.

Aesh could not move himself out of his fetal crouch in the kitchen, elbows on knees and hands clutching his head. He whispered, "I see that I've been vain, thinking I might cure my sterility by making my people fertile."

Ohr bent down so that his head touched Aesh's and whispered back: "I liked your arrogance better than your penitence. Har saved us and you are still the Emperor." Then rose and found a bench, where he could sit with Shemesh on his lap. The Guard did not stop him.

Aesh gradually unfolded himself and sat on the other bench. "How did you get into the root-cellar?"

"Eh. I was standing in the doorway holding Shemesh. A great stupid thing to do, showing the child how Har was cooking our meal, burning it too, and this messenger comes down the street, with an axe, looking like a workman—"

"Here? Those tools are stored at building sites."

"I thought he'd been called out to build something—ptah!" pushing Sefer and his washcloths aside, "Enough! Your rags are catching in my teeth!—and then this axe handler doesn't go by but comes up and swings at Har—"

Har stirred himself and snarled, "I knocked him down with my staff—"

"And this old man here turned back and pushed me and Shemesh under the basin, where I knocked myself out on the edge of it and knew nothing until you howled at me!" He rubbed his head.

"And I finished that one," Har said. "He was no fighter."

The Chief of Guards said to Aesh, "I have questions. You were sure you were not followed last night. But someone knew where you went…"

Aesh said, "This area is always very quiet, and most of the people who live here are too old to work … someone might have followed me last night and hid in the ruins, but would make a deal of noise climbing in and out." He paused to rub his neck, where the muscles had tensed from fear. "I don't believe anyone saw me, or knew where I had gone until I said so in the Council Room, at the table, with only Councillors listening. Do I trust them all, or not? Perhaps one might have been using that messenger, used his wrist comm to send—"

"That is a very big perhaps," the Chief of Guards said.

Aesh noticed that Dos Ramos, who was sitting quietly, had turned very pale, and then flushed, on his forehead and cheekbones. "Forgive me, Dos Ramos, but there are a great many other people from that Council and on this world who would like to see me fail at what they call my 'experiment'. And in these days everyone has a comm on his wrist, I trust you, I can't believe you could ever have been one of them."

"Assassination is a strange task for a messenger," the Chief of Guards said.

"Ah-yah, it is, and he is still lying outside here with an axe in his hand … it may be that he was sent to kill me last night—such a long time ago!—and would have done it if I had not been in the open among the guards in the courtyard, and perhaps if he knew—when he knew where the child was, it seemed even more deadly for him to attack the source, the Father of Mothers."

Ohr said, "It may be that he was not really a messenger, but one hired to look like it. May be and may be. Or not. We know nothing."

"The news he brought is all too true," Dos Ramos said morosely.

༄ ༄

After Shemesh was delivered back to the Hall of Mothers under extra guard, and Har to the nearest hospital, Aesh would have brought his father back to the Council Square to stay with him; but Ohr said, "The guard I swore to hire when you brought me the child will be with me soon, that's enough protection, and it is not likely that anyone will want to kill a retired civil official, so I needn't fear and tremble like a coward." Echoing Aesh's own thoughts about himself. "It is good of you, but I won't eat here with you, I want to be in my own home, even if I burn my meat worse than Har does."

Aesh climbed the tower stair to clean off the wild day's grime and change clothes, but came back down from the bare place to eat once again with the workers at their tables. With the rain gone the clouds had thinned enough so that he could just see, through the thickness of the air, a brilliant line denoting the geosynchronous orbit of the aliens' headquarters and technology laboratories.

As he was finishing the meal he noticed that the Chief of guards was serving himself as well, and turned his head away.

But the guardsman said, "We were lucky today, were we not, Aesh-lord?"

Aesh locked eyes with him. "Yes, we were. Go send word to the Archivist and find out who hired that messenger."

Once more alone in dark space of the tower, he was left with the question: *Why?*

With the hope of restoring women ever shrinking, and Shemesh separated from him perhaps forever, there was nothing to fill the terrifying emptiness in his spirit.

And though he did not believe in the Angry-God, he swallowed a sleeping pellet to stifle his fear that the whole universe might be angry.

· · S I X · ·

RUAH ON FTHEL IV:

S O M E R S A U L T S

She drank deeply from the running stream. The downward course of it made a path for her; looking north now, she could barely see the glint of a window in the heights of the wooded hills above. Back there was food— in a prison.

After a few steps southward hunger struck her. A caved-in feeling not only of hunger for food, but for the closeness of every human of her species that she had lived with in the storms of her godforsaken home world.

She followed the stream and though there were paths that crossed it she did not turn for them. She had no clothing or sandals, and crept from one shadow to the next, a tree limb, a broad leaf, a narrow bridge, so that there was no dark blotch for the aircars buzzing overhead to pick up. She pushed her mind away from the hunger, and gradually became aware of noises she had not made. They were moving in parallel with her: leaves rustling and the crackle of twigs. The air was still.

The stillness disoriented her: her home world was filled with noises, lightning storms and rushing winds. At home people put hands to ears.

Here she listens.

Thinking. *Sneering child with stick. Filthy beggar with knife…*

Big Earther with a stungun and mouth wide open in a howl like the Angry-God joined with all the hurricanes of Barrazan V—

*

—She's out of there—not far enough—

*

he's at her shoulder, swings—

*

—it's the blood in her head roaring now, she's losing strength, a blurry shadow too weak to run, he's grinning at her terror, "Got you!"— raises gun—

*

—now an arm's length away—his hand tightens on the—

*

—she's rolling head over heels, world spinning up and down, up and down, crushing her tail, banging her head on hard ground, and again banging and then her body unrolling itself like a scroll with Angry-God's words on it.

Stopping then, bleary, with cloudy colors in her eyes. She sat up. The *whack!* of the firing gun echoed in her memory, but she was whole. The world was still.

As soon as she got her sight she became aware that the sun was in a different place in the sky. Shadows were longer, the air was warmer. She had gone a distance.

She was crouching on hard and knobby ground, a clearing among trees with bits of stumps in it. Four or five spans away a few people were sitting by a small fire cooking bits of food on sticks. Beyond them the land had been cleared and there were big groups of structures much like the yurts she had lived in at home, and various life forms moving among them. Just in back of her was an electrified fence. She recognized what it was: the hospital had one of those around it. Now she had *shifted* through a second one.

She squatted there, rubbing her head. Then began to shudder and could not stop.

The ones around the fire stared at her: a skinny Earther male, and a much smaller being with tattoos on its head instead of hair, then one more, fat and with a blue skin.

The Earther spoke the same old words:

"Hey-o, what've we got here?"

"Hungry," she said in the same *lingua*. She found herself gnawing her lip.

A hefty Earther woman with one flesh arm and one metal arm came around one of the yurts and stopped in front of her.

Ruah shivered at the sight of that metal arm.

Metal Arm grinned. "Don't worry, dear, I'm not gonna hurt you." She said to the other Earther: "This is a Meshar woman. I've seen them before."

"What's she doing in here, then?"

"What she said—she's hungry."

"We're recruiting fighters here, and she doesn't look like one of them." He stared at her. "Will you fight?

Some spark made her say, "Give me some food and I'll tell you."

He bent over her and clenched his fist. "Don't you joke with me, dog—"

*

"—face!"

Now she was on the other side of the fence, looking in at him. "I guess I am not so hungry now."

"What—"

"Eh, come on, Muggers, I told you, she's a Meshar!"

"I dunno what that is."

"A teleport. She can't *shift* when she wants, only if you frighten her, make her angry, she goes. Through anything, walls, rocks. What's your name, Meshar?"

"Ruah."

"Mine's Grushka. I bet she can fight if she needs to, and you can see she knows how to dodge."

"That'll do *us* a lot of good when we're in the gunsights."

Ruah shrank back. "I am afraid. I want to go home." Everything was happening too quickly and too soon for her.

"They can't send you home from here this minute," the woman said, adding in a low voice, "For God's sake, just tell 'em you'll fight and they'll feed you!"

You are going to kill people ... and be killed. I am hungry ... and there is no way home from here.

"I will fight if I must, then."

"Come on, Muggers, recruiting's what you're paid for, isn't?" She raised and turned her titanium fist, *tick, tock, tick.*

"Awright, we need fighters here and I'll find something for you to eat," the Earther male said. "But if you're gonna jump in and out I'm not wasting food on you. And you," to Metal Arm, "go find Lady Demon here something to wear before she scares the shit out of everybody."

"I think she can eat the bossuk meat we got here. Now you'll have to unlock the gate, Muggers."

The gate opened snarling on its hinges, and let her in.

Muggers stumped off, and Ruah said, "Why are you helping me?"

Metal Arm—Grushka—drew a breath and let it go.

"I'm tired of this bunch of bastards. The place has gotta do good for somebody, and you won't find much more of it here."

DEATH WRACK

Three days went by, slowly for Delius, who went from lodging to crèche, to hive, to hospital and back to lodging. So far his i.d. chip had taken him in and out of quarantine anywhere. He felt lightning flashes of anger crackling from him like a suit of armor, and perhaps they opened doors.

For investigators there were barriers of frustration, and eventually one more room crammed with chairs, benches, desks in variously tormented shapes to suit whatever species were present.

The Shar Kohav and the Meshar Mebarak, in different corners of the room, glanced at each other and looked away into their own distances.

Semdah, the project manager, as well as an Aide to the Administrator General, was an old and majestic Tarrakh who was extremely hairy but not furred; the three diamonds embedded vertically in the center of her high forehead were some kind of clan insigne, Delius thought: they were irregularly cut and not particularly glittering. He always did his best not to think of her as an ancient and very wise baboon, and was grateful there were no telepaths present. With the thought he noticed that she was wearing an impervious net of fine-linked copper chain.

She said in her hushed voice that rustled like silk, "The destruction was carried out by one or more workers who packed explosives into the casings of the monitors in the chamber and set them off by remotes. The worker or workers might be three ten-days gone by now, or even half a year, but we are doing our best to trace them.

"We have no idea whatever why this act took place. The insemination was to be only the first of many experiments that took years to prepare for. But it seems to have been a carefully calculated move—and perhaps even a conspiracy—to stop this project at one particular moment in the most frightening way possible. I can think of nothing to say that would ease the feelings of Kohav or Mebarak."

Kohav said carefully, "What is the use? Mebarak has lost his sisters. My Emperor named my son the Father of Mothers and I have no mate to bring back for him. But if we were to be angry with each other that would only please our enemies."

"I am not angry," Mebarak whispered. "But I will have a lot to answer for at home."

There were murmurs about healing the wounded and searching for the missing, but what Delius sensed most, as if he were a telepath, was a shrinking, even a shriveling in Horrocks.

He left the meeting thinking of Horrocks more than he wanted, perhaps because his mind was so frantic to escape the terror and anger he was living in. He did not linger to speak to anyone.

DOWN: ZAKARIAN

Delius had a free hour and more before the school was let out; he could collect James now … but with Horrocks still on his mind, he found himself walking down the long shadowed hallways with their glimmering lightstrips, and passing the great studded doors of vaster meeting rooms with facilities for species who breathed atmospheres, gaseous or liquid, that even he with all his experience could not imagine. There were few others wandering here in a working hour. He was not usually here either, and he switched off the tracker on his comm.

Above these levels of administrative workers were halls paneled in mother-of pearl and roofed with crystalline arches, where leaders of five thousand worlds argued for their causes and councils debated them almost endlessly, and waited long for judges to rule on them.

Delius had his own kinds of weights and measures. With a twinge of guilt, he went by the schoolrooms and the crèche where the doors were closed and he needn't risk catching the eye of his son, and past empty dining rooms where on-station employees like himself ate. He had now entered the Terrarium, the area in every GalFed quarters that fed and housed Earthers. Every species had a version of home territory.

Just before he reached the branching corridors leading to the lodgings, Delius turned aside and shared space in a freight elevator with a cluster of robot wheelbins, going down. There were more formal routes, but this one was common enough.

Two floors down the Terrarium, floored here with cracked tiles rather than marble slabs, became a shabby area of bars and casinos flickering with coldlights, screens flashing the news of five worlds in thirty-seven languages, the deep purple throbbings of lamps advertising places where women lingered in the evenings behind half-open doors, the usual, all quiet now.

He knew the place well from early years when he had come back to this world with his nerves raveled from dragging colonists out of their homes on dangerous worlds. Like too many Observers, he had no one waiting for him except what he could find in this place; it had not changed much.

Delius passed beyond into one branch of a tree of corridors much like the one upstairs, though the apartments here rented by the hour. He did not stop until he reached the featureless door at the end of the hall, and as he waited there, it opened.

Zakarian, sitting at his desk, was staring at him. "What's it today?"

What else? My life is falling apart. Didn't you know?

Delius was half sure that he must know. Sometimes he wondered if Zakarian operated outside time and space. But though Zakarian knew or could find out almost any secret, he was telepathic only with machines, and not omniscient, though he liked others to believe that.

Delius had a special relationship with him. Years ago they had worked together on many dangerous assignments, until Zakarian decided to quit and invest his brains in inventing and creating electronic devices: some won him great numbers of awards, and others were not completely legal. His on-again-off-again relationship with Galactic Federation was called "Consultant", though there was no title on the door.

"What else? I want information," Delius said. Having been out in the field, he had not visited Zakarian in two or three years, and looked around the windowless, bedroom-sized office to see what had changed. It was the same, but more so. The desk with its thousand touch-tabs might have served an intergalactic warship, and the wall beyond it was now completely paneled with screens that showed scores of private moments; their light cast glimmering colors on Zakarian's round face. He was a small man, and slightly pudgy, without Delius's hidden muscularity. Everything was inside his head; wearing his innocent white shirt, with the tiny silver cross hanging on a fine chain around his neck, something like a gift given to a child; and with his carefully combed and parted brown hair, he looked in some lights like a boy who had grown older without growing up.

The shelves in the wall to his side were crammed with books, tapes, disks, spools, remotes, calculators, hand-helds, e/pads, logic modules and matrixes whose dates ran from yesterday to five hundred years ago. The set of shelves that filled the wall behind him held all the honors and awards that Zakarian had ever won. All were turned inward facing the wall, to show what he thought of the lesser minds who had given them to him.

"I can tell you something for free," Zakarian said. "Someone has tried to murder the father of mothers on Shar—but he's safe, that someone is dead, I'm not telling anyone else and you better not, either. If your crew don't know about that they'll know it soon."

Delius said savagely, "Why didn't you know that everything was going to blow up, then?" and was immediately ashamed.

Zakarian was not stirred. He knew Delius. "I'm not a precog. I can tell you what happened, not what will. Anyway, that's not what you want to know. Spit it."

Somehow Delius could not get the name out of his mouth. *Horrocks.* He had to twist his mouth to say it. "Horrocks. xenobiologist, director of the Xanthrotek project, some first name like 'Wendell.' Claims he's really—"

"Derek Vanbrennan, son of the CEO, Henrik Vanbrennan." Zakarian swirled a finger over the touch-pads and his screens flashed with images of an old man with a thick snubbed nose and a white point of beard. "That may be, but it's also true that his mother, Lillian Wendell Horrocks —gawky name, just like the woman, here she is,"—screen-blink of tall narrow-faced woman with red hair—"wasn't married to the old Vanbrennan. Ever."

"I supposed I shouldn't be surprised."

"Why not? The loyal husband … don't look at me like that, I'm not being sarcastic. You're a bit naïve, you know. But there's more to it…"

Delius found half a seat on the one bare corner of the desk and they stared at each other. He said, "That's a complicated relationship, then. But something is wrong with Horrocks and I'm afraid if he collapses the project will go down the drain for good." *And I and Natya and…*

"I've heard a lot of things…" Zakarian was muttering as if he was telling himself a secret. His face twisted for a moment and he shook his head. "Ah, a long time ago when he was much younger, the father, this old man Vanbrennan, for some crazy reason nobody knows … went to Barrazan Five to consult about terraforming, fell in love … and decided to bring back one of the women—a Meshar…"

"My God, that is more."

Zakarian's mouth twisted. "Of course it was against the law, but he managed to smuggle her out, set up an estate for her on a piece of land he owns down south in the Fire Trees sector. There was a big newsflash over it," Zakarian gestured and the screens swarmed with it, making Delius blink, "that got suppressed of course, and the law conveniently forgot about it too. The woman he'd been going to marry, Lillian, she'd already had his son, she didn't forget."

Delius said with real curiosity, "Why didn't you, Zak? Why keep digging?"

"Because I'm curious, like you! Why else would you be doing this work? And I don't have a wife and kid—forget I said that."

"But Lillian—did she fight him?"

"Vanbrennen settled a lot of his money on the Horrockses and had his son registered as legitimate. So nobody's heard from her since."

"What about the Meshar woman—didn't she have anything to say about being grabbed?"

"What voice would she have had? They could have hit her with a needle-full of the anti*shift*. I guess you know about that, your people use it."

"I don't know all that much, Zak."

"Anyway, her people are alive by GalFed's favor, and I am sure a lot more money was being spread around."

"Horrocks is certainly loyal to his father. I can see why he's so upset, but—"

Zakarian said, "I heard—this is just a rumor—I heard old Henrik was trying to find a way to get a child on that woman, the Meshar. Had to give it up, of course. All of Xanthrotek couldn't do that—and wouldn't ever try … maybe that's why they're working so hard to reconstruct the Shar, stop them from becoming toys for aliens."

"Horrocks was telling me he loved those seven Meshar women. And he said, quote, 'That doesn't mean I wanted to fuck them.' Do you think he could have been helping his father try…"

"You know him better than I do. What do you think?"

"There's enough reason for him to have mixed emotions. I don't know him enough to tell … but the old man must be really crazy. How can he run the company?"

"He doesn't, really. There's a big lot of directors that pretends to follow his orders."

"That's hard on Horrocks. Whose orders does he follow?"

"You're the Observer, Delius."

"Eh, Horrocks is a hard worker. Trying to impress the old man. But he wouldn't do anything so gross a helping him create a chimera."

Delius did not know how Zakarian lived, and imagined a narrow cot in a tiny room—untouched by human hands, might be the words. Little or nothing of the animal, there. *And of course I might be entirely mistaken.* There was a limit to what he understood. But in other ways he and Zakarian knew altogether too much about each other. "What do I owe you?"

"I'll ask when I need it. Oh, and you, keep a good eye on your wife and kid."

Delius stood looking at him.

"The kid's safe in the crib, and your wife's fine for the moment, but you know about giving hostages…"

"There's not many other ways to give and get love, Zak."

Always when he left Zakarian Delius had the feeling that there was so much more that Zakarian knew and did not tell. And as always he was not sure that he wanted to have that kind of knowledge.

FOR THE MOMENT

If you wanted you could make up a story about Lillian Wendell Horrocks and her son … the jealousy and rage that must have festered all the years— or did it? "Nobody's heard from her since…"

But: could she be using her son to smash her lover, murder a child, make a sick world worse? Is that real? Even thinkable? Is that what Horrocks is afraid of? Or … "I don't mean I wanted to fuck them," he said. *Does he really know what his father wanted so much? How could he not?*

A yank on his hand from James, who was jumping up and down as they walked the corridors: "Is Mum still in that awful place? I ask and ask, and you aren't listening!"

Keep a good eye … "Easy, easy, Jimbo! We'll go see."

"Come on, then!"

A good eye. An indirect threat to himself? In the field he and Zakarian had saved each other's lives.

Now again the moving walkways carried Delius and his son through the tunnels under the glaring lightstrip, in the same silence as had bound them both in the morning.

And only one twenty-five hour day since James had told him of the Meshar woman. The news of explosion. The painful meeting with Mbai. The accusation. And now there was Zakarian's news of more terror on Shar. And Delius was sure his superiors knew of that, he did not need to tell them. *Safe,* Zakarian had said.

In its warped way the one round of hours seemed to Delius almost as long as the time since he began his long voyage to Shar, when he had left James as a toddler and come back to find him a schoolboy.

꿔꿪

The i.d. chip took him and the boy past the sentinels of the quarantined multiplex. The translucent walls of Natalya's room showed him a dark blurred figure there, and his heart jumped, but when the door swung open he found only Dr. Mukherjee, her long-time associate, sitting beside her.

The crackling force-field had been turned off, and some of Natalya's bandages had been replaced with collagen sealers, so that the wounds on her scalp and shoulder looked more ugly than terrifying. Splintered glass, Delius thought. Half of her hair had been sheared off. But her eyes were open and alert.

Mukherjee had not escaped injury: he had one arm in a sling and also a swath of collagen up the bloody side of his neck and jaw. But he was still ambulatory, and rose to leave.

Delius said, "Please don't get up for me I don't mind waiting outside."

"No, no! I was only holding the place for you." Mukherjee smiled faintly, and then: "Everything has become so strange in just a few hours."

"Yes, it has."

"I will make sure they take good care of her."

"Take care of yourself," Delius said, sensing the depth of Mukherjee's sadness. He did not yet have the heart to ask about the other Meshar women.

Natalya reached out a hand to hug James and said, "Half of my hair is gone."

"You'll comb it over," Delius said, and kissed her. And kissed her again. Grateful to have James along, so that they were together, and wanting to be alone with her in their bed, whispering into the darkness.

꿔꿔

DEPTH

…here is Henrik Vanbrennan, pulling himself up out of the darkness. Opening her door, watching as she sleeps, with her sweet breath moving in small currents…

Delius jumped out of sleep in a bursting sweat. At the same time there was a thundering *CRUMP* beneath the floor and the walls shuddered and rumbled.

He sat shivering. James, for all his nerves, was a hearty sleeper and did not stir.

There were murmurs in the halls, and a guard's voice calling, "Nothing happening here! Go back to sleep, people!"

Delius did not want to return to that dream, but nothing he might dream now would comfort him.

꿔꿔

In the morning he was in his cubicle, gulping coffee to keep his gritty eyes open and trying to pick up on the reports he had been compiling for the last quarter year on his voyages to the Shar and the Meshar. Thinking that all of this work might be useless and forgotten, along with the Shar and the Meshar.

And dreading the next call to one of those meetings, when Genever stopped by. Delius did not like the look on his face, but that was not for the first time.

Genever said, "You'll be interested to know what happened last night."

"Will I? What'sit, then?" Delius said mildly, blinking at the screen in front of him.

"There was an explosion two floors down."

Delius suppressed his shiver and said, "Sounded like it."

"Yes. Security were afraid the walls would collapse, but they built it well here. No hint of what it's about."

Delius raised his eyes and stared into Genever's pink and shiny face. "Was anybody hurt?"

"Eh, it was in that apartment at the end of the corridor—didn't your friend Zakarian live there?—if he was in there—"

Delius wanted to swing that iron bar of an arm.

"Of course I'm sorry, but if it hadn't blasted the door off first it might have collapsed a wall, and everything in there was—"

Delius stood up and said, "That's enough, Genever."

Genever shrank back with his hands raised in a don't-kill-the-messenger gesture and sidled off.

Delius sat down and stared at the display before him, items, asterisks, symbo*lingua.*

Everything has become so strange in just a few hours, Mukherjee had said.

Zakarian was almost the only old friend he had been able to keep up with in all those years out on alien worlds.

Dead or alive, no. Dead. Unless ... he had so many tricks. But nobody could have lived through that. With his screens and medals and all that tech-nojunk. He knew too much, the old cliché, you damned idiot, you knew more

than you told me, or I'd be dead too. And I asked for all that. And there's no
escaping this place.

James in the crèche up the hall and Natalya down the long dark walkway.

THE WORLD SHAR:

CAPITAL CITY EQUATORIAL LANDS

In a morning that was already beginning to cloud over, Aesh Seven stood at the head of the stairs trying to will himself to go down and have breakfast at the trestle tables in the courtyard, as he had done so often lately; he liked the workers, who were goodnatured and not afraid to speak out in his presence. Now everything weighed heavy on his head: a council meeting where his aching spirit was too tired for him to press his arguments; more challenges from Givor, where he must not let himself shrink—

The step on the stairway, now, that might be anyone…

But he knew that it was Dos Ramos, who wore boots and not clogs, and Sefer had already announced him. No enemy.

A pause at the top of the stairway. "Dos Ramos? Will you come in?" Something wrong there.

Dos Ramos came in slowly. His face was flushed. The way aliens worked, shame or anger. Perhaps both.

Aesh raised his hand, palm up. "Say it."

Dos Ramos said in a hoarse voice, "I have been called back," he lifted his head, "up there, or perhaps to Earth. My employers claim that I have been behaving improperly by trying to help you, by carrying a weapon, and…" he shrugged and sighed—

"—I understand," Aesh said. "Not keeping the proper distance from the alien."

"Please!"

"I'm not blaming you, Dos Ramos. But I wonder whose hand and voice are in control here."

No longer mine, evidently.

"Aesh-lord, the world belongs to the people who live in it. I don't want to be the *alien* to you, but evidently I have been considered faulty, perhaps not alien enough in the eyes of others. And I wish you well alongside whoever comes next."

"Dos Ramos, nobody is coming next, today. I want you at the Council meeting, not someone else."

"Aesh-lord, I will be safer if I don't disobey orders."

"Come for a moment and let us wish you well at least."

Aesh listened to the steps fading downward.

Sefer called, "Are you coming down, lord?"

"Yes…" He paused. "But Sefer…?"

Sefer was looking up at him, about to say something, raised a hand, then quickly lowered it.

"What is it, Sefer? Come up."

"You will not like—"

"You too?" Aesh held out his hands. "Say it anyway, it's troubling you."

Sefer pursed his lips for a moment, and said, "Aesh-lord, I don't trust Givor. He pretends kindness, but gives his servants very little." He took a step back and seemed to shrink.

Aesh said very quietly, "You know of this." A statement.

"I was one."

"An unhappy man, perhaps, even with all those sons." Three of them he knew of, and none of those other … ones.

"He wants to be emperor."

"One day he may be, and I wish him well of that."

And what can I do about that? Shall I take him from his sons and send him to the Polar Territories? Send the lot of them?

"Wait for me downstairs. I'm coming down in a moment."

He looked up at the frieze of men, women, children dancing over the walls. *Did they really ever exist? Or was Kessev Five a madman with a dream?* Before he went down the stairs, he opened a cupboard door and found on a shelf an old bronze shoulder clasp he had worn as he was becoming an adult, and tucked it into the crease in his leather tunic that served as a pocket.

He glanced upward once more. Givor as Emperor in this tower. A vision of mallets smashing—

He took the bronze clasp from his pocket and placed it back on the shelf.

The clerks, messengers, servants in the courtyard greeted him with the same goodwill but were not, he felt, quite so talkative, and seemed to move more slowly—or perhaps his mind and body were what moved slowly. They murmured, "Lord," offered him food, and he took it with appreciation, but did not speak much more.

゛ア゙ド゙

Across the Council table Aesh faced the lot of them among the red bars of sunlight as they met his eyes or avoided them, red-black, red-black, some black streaked with white scars of age, like Arvig's; Givor whacking his tail against the bench leg with impatience, dim-eyed Arvig with yellowish age-streaks in his fur and whitened guardhairs, good to have for a friend, though his mind often wandered far, and his son Ayin … Dos Ramos's chair was unoccupied. No aliens here today.

For a moment Aesh wished once more that he had a majestic

presence like his father. But when he told his father of his election to Emperor, Ohr had said, *Better you than me.*

❧❦

In the earliest years of his office, the consortium of aliens had invited Aesh to visit them in their vast city-in-orbit, and Ohr's advice then had been, *Be respectful, but don't lick their feet.*

He recalled the tremendous force of the lift, and how fiercely he had had to control himself, knowing what weaknesses his hosts were expecting to find in him.

They led him into a room lined with dials, controls, switches, drew him to the great porthole of strange thick glass, to look down at the dark fogged world flickering with lightnings, and told him: "There you are, lord of all you see!" He had learned quickly how to read their expressions.

Where was the voice in his head that should have been saying: *Listen to them with the greed bubbling up in their throats?*

The voice said: *Food. Metals. Forges. Water to drink.*

"I'm not any lord, sirs, only a man chosen by his people." *And by you, don't think I don't know it. Aiyah! Look at that home of mine down there! Surely Angry-God made that.*

❧❦

He sat for a moment, to take possession of his bench, then stood up to face his Council and said, in a voice of careful neutrality: "I know that our member Dos Ramos has been called back by his employers, but I asked him to come at least for this sitting, so that we may wish him well." He addressed the recording secretary. "Has he decided not to come?"

"I believe he said that he would come, Aesh-lord."

"There is no need to wait for him," Givor said.

"I agree," Aesh said calmly. "If he chooses to come, he's—"

From the courtyard one hoarse gasping cry came, then a clatter of spears, and Sefer appeared in the doorway with a streak of blood down the side of his head, his guardhairs standing up like spines.

Aesh jumped up so quickly that his bench crashed to the floor. Sefer spat blood and said, "He."

Aesh ran, but not soon enough. Dos Ramos was lying dead just inside the gate, in his back the bolt of a crossbow standing in a red eye of blood. Nothing to be done.

Crossbow? None of his guards in the courtyard used crossbows. "Sefer? What—"

"He—that one with the bow, he shot through the bars of the gate, twice, I tried…"

Aesh cried, "You, guard! Take Sefer to the physician! And stay with him!"

And with a long drawn breath, "All of you out here! You are guards, out in the full sun, and you are here to watch! Is there no one who saw anything!" He snarled, "And where are you, Chief of Guards?"

The guards dropped their spears and turned their heads aside in shame. Far across the courtyard, the Chief Guard stood like stone.

Aesh squatted beside Dos Ramos, hands on knees … found himself whispering, "Friend … friend…" Eventually he let one of the guards draw him back into the Council Chamber.

The frame of his bench had broken. Someone brought him another.

He rarely believed in omens, but this was not a good one.

FTHEL IV:
Ruah in the state of bonzador

The hills were low here, and the weather did not change twenty times a day. Every day people ate three times, and there was rain between the second and third meals. Everyone wore the same clothing, a coverall made from a pulpy stuff, like the nests of the segneb worms in the jungles of her home world, marked with designs of tree branches; and everybody lived in tents made of the same material, only thicker.

She was used to living in tents: her people carried their heavy leather yurts for half of the days looking for places where the trees were not falling, or lightning striking them, or volcanoes flinging their hot ashes everywhere.

But here there were many more strange animals than even her world held. Maybe more of those than people. She had scarcely enough time to put on the dreadful crackling tunic before one of them came up to her: a powerful red-furred beast far too large for any tunic, with much longer fangs and claws than her own, who stared at her with huge red eyes that flashed green as she moved.

"Don't worry," this beast growled in rough *lingua.* "I am not eating you."

She felt, suddenly, as if her brains had turned to water.

"Yes, I am a telepath, and you must become used to me, because we are sleeping in the same tent. Likely because we both have fur. My name is Rrengha, and I am Ungrukh. That is, an Ungrukh woman."

She digested the information with some difficulty and found a small voice, finally: "Are you here to fight with all the others? And are all these here really people?"

"They believe they are. Some of them don't believe I am people, but they learn." She added a lash of her tail, for emphasis. "And fighting? We learn about that soon enough."

Some rough voice called for them to get to work, and she found that work, here and now, meant clearing away the thorny brush that swarmed over the dry clay soil. The trees here were thin weak things, faint shelter from the brassy sun. Rrengha fitted instruments over her claws to give herself something like fingers, and went to find some task for herself; the more Ruah observed her, the less she feared her, and the more "human" everyone else looked, even the one with six limbs.

Overseers yelled at the workers that were supposed to be "fighters," "Faster, you lumping juddars, faster! Get that brush on the loaders!" until the rains began to fall with great force, and then everyone crawled away into the dripping tents. But if she had little fear of all these ones beside her, she was suddenly twisted with homesickness so vicious it might have been an animal itself.

"Hullo, Ruah! Come and eat." Here now, after the rains, was Grushka, the cheerful woman with the metal arm. Home was here now.

And what else might be here? *Ones that want to poke me with sticks? Ones that want to fuck me or eat me, or kill me with that gun?* And the night was worse, not for danger but for that hot and hugely snoring body beside her; still, in spite of it all she was not quite so lonely. All those that came at her had been Earthers. And this one with the fur did not want to eat her. Yet.

HAPPY FAMILIES AND OTHERS

Delius stared at the screen trying to reach a calm area somewhere in his mind where the attack on the Meshar women would fit alongside the attempt to kill the child on Shar and the death of Zakarian. Zakarian would not have killed himself, not when everything he loved best was within arm's reach. Would he?

And why did I go to him, anyway, risk being tracked and stirring up suspicion? Why worry about Horrocks, a name as gawky as the man who wore it, like his mother.

But Horrocks had been in agony. Fearfully vulnerable, and without him the painstaking coordination of the project might not have been possible.

And what did Zak tell me? A family history, and not much to it at that. Mother and son over here, father on some other square of the board … or some other arrangement of three game pieces.

He thought of his own parents, both diplomats, stately columns of marble, who had brought him up straight no matter how much he wanted to zigzag. Eventually he had been forced to learn how to do that on all those dangerous worlds with their angry colonists, and he had freed himself, almost.

He went over in his mind the half hour with Zakarian, only half an hour. And any moment now there would be a meeting of people who wanted to know what he had to do with that secretive man. Mbai pestering and Genever smirking.

But he kept going back to that half hour, pushing at his memory to lay down the words on the surface of his mind.

"Derek Vanbrennan, son of the CEO," Zakarian says. "That may be, but it's also true that his mother, Lillian Wendell Horrocks—gawky name, just like the woman, here she is"—screen-blink of tall narrow-faced woman with red hair—"wasn't married to the old Vanbrennan. Henrik. Ever…"

Image of Vanbrennan, the non-scientist CEO: an old man with a thick snubbed nose and a white point of beard.

Son of the CEO? That may be, says Zakarian.

Tall, gawky, red-haired narrow-faced Horrocks, a male image of his mother. *"You're kind of naïve, you know."*

Not quite that much, Zak. Could he have been murdered just to hide that tiny grain of knowledge if that was true? That Horrocks was not the son of the CEO? Probably not, but something to think about.

Or not. It could be some other reason, entirely.

You do too damned much deep thinking, Delius, says Genever. *Zak? Did you really get blown up?*

But it did not seem possible that he could not summon Zakarian's childish face to his screen. *Dead?*

His comm buzzed with staccato insistence.

Here it comes.

HEAVY, HEAVY

Perhaps she found being a Project Manager unbearable at times: Semdah wore so many alien expressions on her wrinkled primate's face that it was difficult for any other alien to read it, and they made the diamonds on her forehead glitter strangely. She was crouched at her desk twisting the copper impervious net in her hands. A mind open to everything. Slowly and deliberately she raised the helmet and fitted it over her head.

"Mbai is a good worker, but overworked. She would not, what you call, 'pester' you."

"I didn't know we had thought-police now." Delius strove, as always in her presence, to keep his own face straight. He owned but did not wear a helmet. It scratched his head, and he felt it dulled his mind.

"Things have changed since you've been away, Delius, but nobody can imprison you for what you think. That law still holds good."

Semdah did not live in the hive but had her own small world, walled with panels that looked like wood, and floored with carpeting woven out of many-colored reeds. Something like the ones the Shar used. She wore a shoulder wrap of luminous threads that picked up the colors of the floor. In one corner of the room there were game boards of several worlds, set with ranks of onyx and marble hexagons and chess pieces, as well as a hinged go-ban with pots of black and white stones set on it. Delius wondered if the wall panels might unfold into a bed, a basin, a wardrobe, and make a home. Because the room fitted Semdah, the way that darkened cube had done for Zakarian.

Semdah said, "The loss of Zakarian is most unfortunate. As any is, and particularly because he was so useful to us, and of course we had already known most of what he told you. It may sound strange to you, but I had hoped that explosion was one more scarperer's trick of Zakarian's and he had escaped, but the analysis of the matter in that place…"

"Maybe there were still one or two things he knew that somebody wanted to make sure never came to light."

"Perhaps. The fragment of the good in that tragedy is that it was so public, so we needn't investigate it in secrecy."

"I don't know if Zak would appreciate that."

"You are not implicated, and I am sure he would appreciate that. Your contact with him was somewhat risky—for you—because everyone has been so disturbed here, and each one of us is always being tracked. But only I and Rosa Mbai know of that visit, and I admit that she was angry, partly at me for esping, but I could not have been sure about you otherwise, and told her to be still."

"I'm grateful for your trust," Delius said, and meant it in spite of his resentment at her spying. *What I've been doing most of my life.*

"No, you have been trustworthy for many years, and never took advantage of information as Zakarian did. He lived for risk and secrets, and he was very useful, but he had many enemies.

"As for Horrocks, he may not know the relationships of his parents, but he will have to pull himself out of his funk, because we need his ability to deal with Shar and Meshar, and we have nothing to say that could help him…" Delius knew that Horrocks had a subdermal helmet, and Semdah could not esp him.

"But listen, Delius. I want you to work quickly and finish your reports. We need field operatives for this work now, and there are—"

Delius felt a rush of blood to his face. "Are you trying to get rid of me? I'm damned if I'm going to leave my wife and son here in danger—"

"Calm down, Delius, for Holy Aagar's sake! I do understand how you feel with your wife wounded, and having to look out for your son. We will keep them safe one way or another. I swear to that as you swore to Aesh Seven, though I have no Stone to put my hand on."

She rose and picked a pawn off the chessboard, held it up for a moment, then flipped it into its box. "Did you know an Earther named Salvador Dos Ramos?"

"Yes, I've worked with him."

"He was working for Xanthrotek on Shar. But he's ours. He gave strength to Aesh, we sent him out there for that. And he's dead."

"How do you know that?"

"We have a plant with one of the other orbiters, but no one must know who that one is."

"And do you know who killed Dos Ramos?"

"No, but it was a Shar using a crossbow. I know there are many Shar who don't want whole women. And I'm sure there are exploiters among the aliens in orbit who are happy to see the Shar with a low birthrate. But I don't know if there was any connection with what's been happening here. All the same it looks to me as if that move was an attack on Aesh."

"What do you expect me to do there, Director? Be the god-like alien who descends to create order? I'm an Observer, and this is no work for one of that kind!"

"Because you've done that work so well, you're the alien closest to Aesh Seven, and we need you to be the authority figure there."

"I've spent my whole life hiding that part of myself!"

"But It Is there inside you, Delius, and I believe anyone who knows you would agree with that. Now...

"The *Zarandu of Thanamar* is orbiting us, and it will stay in orbit here for the next thirtyday at least. Then it will ship out to Shar and its sibling worlds to deliver supplies and load those ingots the worlds love so much ... I don't believe Aesh has very many friends on that world, Delius."

"My wife and son—"

"I will guard them with my life."

Strangely, he believed her.

"Over Shar, the ship will have a thirtyday's orbit and that will probably not be enough time to do much. But you must do what you can for Aesh, if he is still alive, and even if he is not, his enemies must feel our eyes on them. If you have to stay longer, the *Aleksandr Nevskii II* will be arriving within the next thirtyday and bring you back here. If necessary we will demand that the orbiting community that sucks on the world bring you back." *Dead or alive*, she did not say. "You will have enough risk pay then to do whatever you want, retire, travel, work anywhere else among the inhabited worlds."

"You've planned it all out for me," Delius said with some bitterness.

"Yes. You can refuse, and we will find someone else. But you swore to Aesh Seven, Delius. You made the promise."

"I also swore that I would not tell."

"Nor have you told. I have illegally taken the information from you, for good or evil … and it is barely possible that you may be able to save Aesh Seven's life."

She looked hard at him, and the diamonds glittered like eyes in her forehead. "I know everything," she said, half whispering. "My one child, my daughter, traveled far away to save someone and died on a knifepoint. I thank **h**oly Aagar that it wasn't I that sent her. You were out on those worlds, Delius, as an Observer, and alone, and you know how it was—and now, with all the efforts we have made for Shar women, all blasted away, you are tired of everything to do with this work.

"But those Shar have suffered on that world for endless years, and they have made themselves a civilization in spite of everything. We must do something for them. Will you help save them, Delius?"

"You'd better swear that if I die you'll take care of Natya and the boy," Delius said. "All their lives."

"I have sworn."

"I want to take Kohav with me."

"You may take Kohav if he agrees, and some of that crew who were supervising on the first trip. They know how to handle themselves as well as you do. Not Genever, no matter what the God Xanthrotek may say—"

"And Horrocks?"

"Horrocks is too unstable … useful as he is I'm unwilling to risk him, and I can think of a good replacement. Eh, a last thing! On this visit you are an emissary, Delius, not a secret agent or a mere aide. If they even threaten you, they will regret it very much."

Much good their regret will do me. Delius rose, and felt the weight of his body as if it were the world.

"And Delius … I pray you have no enemies…"

Delius said, "If I have I'm sure they realize that I don't know everything Zakarian knew."

"Perhaps. But it's my ears will be slit if it goes wrong."

PARENTHOOD

Delius did not go back to the hive, but instead collected James from the crèche.

"Why did you come for me early?" James did not really mind missing a spelling test.

"We're going to visit Mother."

The boy's hand tightened on Delius's. "Is something wrong?"

"No, I just want to talk to her, because I might have to go…" More words that were hard to speak.

"Away from us?"

"For a short time."

"Where? Where?"

"We'll talk to Mother first, and you'll know too."

The small hand tightened further. "I have the right to know now! You've been away so much, and you've only just come back!"

That was true, and the words were bitter in his mouth. "I might have to go to the world Shar."

"Where all those people live? That person I saw in the park was one of them, you said she was a Shar, she had red and black eyes that were scary. And three tits. And the way she blinked out." He shivered. "I don't like her."

"That was a Meshar woman, she was one of a group that broke away from the Shar and got to live somewhere else. You just have to get used to whoever you see around here." Delius marveled now to find himself holding the boy's hand and talking in a fairly sensible voice, while the walkway slid and the light swelled and ebbed overhead.

It's my ears will be slit, says Semdah. Even she had someone who spoke to her in a voice like falling stones.

"I like most of the people here," James said.

"Good."

"Not that Thornberg kid who wanted to stick her."

"Right. I'll let you dislike him."

༉༠

Delius saw through the frosted walls that the small hospital room was already filled with visitors … and the darkness of the three figures in green tunics was that of Meshar women. James went rigid but Delius kept a tight hold on him. He stood in the doorway.

Natalya was propped up on pillows, the remaining half of her hair tied back neatly. The three Meshar had obviously disregarded the uncomfortable chairs and were squatted before her in an arc with their knees up and tails curled around their feet. They were speaking, mainly all three at the same time, in broken bits of *lingua* supplemented with wild and expressive gestures, as Natalya did her best to reply in scraps of their own language.

The room's atmosphere, with all of the lilting voices, was peaceful, and Delius stood watching them, and felt the boy gradually relaxing beside him.

After a moment Natalya looked up, smiling. Delius smiled back, and said, "I'll come back after dinner, and we'll talk."

But the Meshar women turned shy and slipped away; then he and James were left with no way to delay what had to be spoken. James said, "Dad has to tell you—"

Delius said quickly, "I'll tell her. Go out in the hall for a minute, James. Where I can watch you."

He turned to Natalya. The smile had faded and she had that expression ... "You're going away. I don't know where, but you're going."

She knew him. His mouth was stiff. "I was ordered."

"Yes? The rest of us are abandoned here in the great secret enterprise where everything is smashed, the way I've been smashed, nobody knows who did all of this, nothing's been found out—"

"I made a promise—"

"Yes, you'll promise anybody in the universe—"

"I'll never leave you again, ever."

"Yes, yes, if there's anything left of me and this place!" She turned her face away.

"You'll be cared for, and guarded." She had no answer; she was so small, crouched in the bed-clothes, and so fierce. He added, "You've made promises too, when we came here. I wouldn't have come without you. You'll be out of bed in a day or two and back at work—"

"And what of you, a light-year away with a thousand knives aimed at you, the way it's always been?"

"I'll do my best to come back with a whole skin. You've got to admit, I've always managed that."

She turned her head and withered him with a look.

He sighed. "If I go you'll hate me, and if I don't go I'll hate myself. Is that how it has to be?"

"Being angry is one thing and hate is another," she said quietly. "I'll never hate you."

"Then … a kiss, now … please, let me have a kiss?"

She gave him the kiss.

꿔꿔

James did not ask what that was all about. "Mother looks better."

"Yes … I'm glad of that." Dark red track running down the side of her face, over her shoulder, zigzagging along her upper arm like a lightning bolt, strangely gleaming with the sealer.

James added grudgingly, "I guess those Meshar don't look frightening."

"They do look frightening to lots of people, and that's why it's hard to get help for them when they need it."

"But you're going away. Again."

"To help. I made a promise," he said again. *Damned promises.*

That night both of them slept deeply. James with relief to see his mother healing, Delius from exhaustion. But before he slept he thought deeply about Zakarian. Probably the man was dead. But he was not as sure as Semdah that he was not playing "one more scarperer's trick."

* * E I G H T * *

CAPITAL CITY EQUATORIAL LANDS

Aesh sat frozen for a long moment, staring at the red bars of sunlit dust, while the body of Dos Ramos was taken away. Then he said to the nearest guard, "I want to see the Chief of Guards."

The Chief of Guards came, moistening his lips.

"You've had words to say to me," Aesh said. "Now you tell me what you were doing when that killer came with his crossbow."

The Chief Guard spoke steadily: "There was a fight that broke out in the northeast corner between two men I know well, about a spear or staff that got broken. They have served many years."

"Leave ten days' pay off them. Now send those that were guarding within the fence in here, so I can question them, and after that take two others out with you to guard in their place. And don't let anyone come or go." He twisted to face the lot of those thirty-nine around him and said in the same quiet voice, "You have no objections."

None were spoken.

But the guards had nothing to add: the bowman had appeared as Dos Ramos was stepping on the lintel, let fly once, to kill, again to graze Sefer's head, and vanished.

One of them said, "There are some of them that can *shift* to come and go as they like, Aesh-lord."

Aesh knew of them, and they were very few. Most were professional fighters in travelling fairs, and the rest were felons who did not last long, because they gradually lost the sense of landing that kept them out of deep waters or stone walls.

"You may go," Aesh told the guards.

"I would have held on to those ones," old Arvig said, "and twisted their thumbs for them."

"I am not a thumb-twister," Aesh said, "and Dos Ramos would still be dead." With a heavy breath he said, "I want to find out from the Archivist the record of that messenger who nearly killed my father and the child. The Archivist is not here?"

The recording secretary said timidly, "No, Aesh-lord, he's home in North Hills with a broken shoulder from falling off his doorstep."

Aesh grunted and found himself wordless.

Givor said harshly, "So far everything we have tried to do to restore the female of our people has come to nothing! Now this alien is dead and we may be blamed for it. Your father and the child were nearly killed. Why waste time and effort lowering ourselves to lick the feet of aliens who do nothing but suck our world's wealth and despise us!"

"If our people was whole again we would not be so despised, and the healing is something we must do whether we have help or not."

"I don't need women, I have my sons! I have my sons! What more do I need in my life but my sons and the sons of my sons!"

"But who would want to take them away from you? Would you think it was some manner of sin to give them women for mates?"

"I know, I know that there would be anger and contempt for those who don't want to change!"

"When I was coming in here I heard someone calling outside the wall, 'Angry-God destroyed Woman because she was foul and evil!' Do you believe that?"

"How could I? The only kind of woman I have seen was the one that gave me my sons."

There was very little to give answer to those words. But the answers he could not give ricocheted in Aesh's mind in back of the vision of Dos Ramos lying dead:

You, Givor, you can afford to hire other men to give their lives to tending, feeding and cleaning those unwomen as well as your sons while you sit at the Council table, you are free to enjoy your sons while laborers without wealth or power have to work and take care of their children and of those helpless ones ... women would at least help...

How do I know what women would do? On those walls in my tower there are perfect women and perfect children. Could I prove that fleshly women would be more loving? Not beat their servants? Sit at this Council table and make wiser decisions?

'Eh, bad luck that you are sterile, Aesh-seed. If you had had children you would have known much more...'

More of what, Ohr-father? Perhaps I would have my sons as Givor does. But God is not loving in our part of the universe.

All that Aesh could see now whether his eyes were closed or open, was the image of Dos Ramos lying dead with the bolt in his back and that ring of blood around it.

He said, "You are right, we are making no progress. But I refuse to give up the hope of restoring the women in our world. I still want to know who that messenger was who tried to kill us, and why. And my friend, Dos Ramos, who made the mistake of trying to do me a favor and stayed too long..."

Old Arvig cried, "I know of nobody on this world who would have begrudged you that!"

"Neither do I, but one of 'us' did kill him." He stood. "There's nothing more for us to say now."

At the end of the southwestern wing of the Council house, beyond the empty chapel, there was a small one-storey building of rough stone that looked like an afterthought. There were latrines here, closets for mops and brooms, and a small office kept by the physician, and assisted every few days by a visit from one or other of the alien doctors who served the miners or desalination plant workers.

The current alien was a slender and hairless Bengtvadi whose smooth tan skull was heavily tattooed with clan markings. Both he and the attendant Shar greeted Aesh with reassurances. The Shar doctor was wearing a blue-green hemp-cloth tunic like his patient, but the Bengtvadi was resplendent in a burnt orange ceremonial robe; the intensity of the heat did not bother him. Aesh knew and trusted both of these men.

Sefer was sitting up, heavily bandaged on one side of the head, and his eyes were full of pain.

The Bengtvadi said, "It is not so much that he hurts, but that he is reproaching himself." He spoke the local dialect with a melodious voice impossible for a Shar.

"I should have saved him," Sefer growled.

"Short of grasping the bolt and pulling it out of the air, I can't see how," Aesh said. "You acted most bravely and bravery doesn't always succeed."

"Do you still want me for your guard?"

The Bengtvadi raised a hand, but Aesh said, "Yes, but not tonight. You come when Doctor says so."

It seemed to him that he read a thought in Sefer's eyes—or perhaps only in his own imagination, but…

This Bengtvad is one you'd best not try to make a friend of, Aesh-lord, if you want to keep him alive.

After he had stepped out into the courtyard, he recalled that the Bengtvadi were telepaths—low-grade and unobtrusive, but telepaths.

He spent the rest of the day in the usual meetings with employees, committees, alien representatives pretending to consult him, secretaries taking records on clay tablets. The scientists did not come. Perhaps they had given up trying to produce mothers.

Arvig had the grace to invite him to share a meal, but the old man would tell too many old stories he knew already, and he ate supper again with the guards in the courtyard, though they avoided his eyes. He helped them clear the trestles and sat down on a bench looking up at the sky that was greyish as always without wind or rain. Trying to find a space in his mind where he might rest.

The Chief of Guards kept lingering not far away as darkness rose in the east, and remained when the others went to quarters and the night guards came to replace them. Aesh said, "Why are you staying here?"

This watchman was a bold one. Squatting on his haunches, settling his belly between them, he said without blinking, "I want to make sure you are safe this time."

"Ayeh! I'm safe the way a prisoner is safe."

"That's what you pay for being Emperor."

"Arvig thinks I should have twisted your thumbs for disobedience and impudence."

"You docked those two fools ten days' pay."

"They will still have food. It won't hurt them to smoke less dirtweed."

"There's none of that here! I make sure of it."

"Are you saying I should have done more?"

"Told them to get out."

"Eh, and you told me they were faithful servants!"

The Chief Guard was unabashed. "I am not the emperor."

"Then they would have had to find work taking care of womb-bearers instead of being guards of the Emperor."

"Aesh-lord, I am guarding you here at night when I don't need to, to show that you have the power of the Emperor. If someone had killed you, the Emperor, you would be pitied as a hero of sacrifice, and that would be the end of everything you are trying to do. I am helping you to be respected."

"You sound like my father. Guarding me you are also saving yourself from a real punishment. Watchman, this moment I'm tired of being Emperor. Sleep well."

❧

He writhed and tossed on his bedding. And his mind stormed and would not let him drift.

Why was he killed?

Because he was my friend. Willing to remain my friend he showed signs of disloyalty to those that hired him, the ones that want some other emperor. Am I guilty of trying to keep him as a friend? I asked no more of him, or the ones who hired him, but that he be allowed to attend our meeting one more time.

"My employers claim that I have been behaving improperly by trying to help you."

Was the order to kill given by someone in our Council, or someone in the orbit? If I had only just let him go. No. I'm sure he knew too much about something I don't know … why else kill him?

Knowing nothing, having no real power … why be Emperor? Why restore females? I am sterile. Why—

Twisting in an agony of desperation and bitterness, he
*

found himself in a brawling night street filled with late-waking crowds who stank of the grindbrew. Rain began drizzling. Lightning cracked the sky and thunder echoed over it.

Not a dream. Aesh had *shifted* only two or three times in his life and this one was as dizzying as the rest.

There were no lovers clasping hands affectionately, no troops of children in this street, learning about their work in the future, the care of womb-bearers, but on each side there was a long line of the stone halls where the unwomen lay. He knew where he was, at the northernmost point of the city. There were attendants here, but no guards bearing crossbows. And no peacefulness here.

The night shift was coming off duty, rolling smokes out of their sling-pockets and lighting them with wooden matches.

Two or three people gaped at Aesh and muttered among themselves: "Forgot to put on his clothes, he has! Wonder what he wants?"

"Hasn't got much to offer."

He was only too conscious now that he had no clothes, or clogs to walk on, and shrank back against a wall, shivering, with his guardhairs standing out like spikes, and now jogged by the gapers who yelled, "Look at those over there!" "Those" were a pair going by, with blue-painted faces and buttocks, holding each other up, staggering drunk, and howling old hymns to Angry-God in outland accents; another screeching pair with red and yellow patches followed after, mock-humping; probably most of them were performers coming off a late show in some grog hall, going after their own pleasures.

The group around Aesh pointed at him and yelled at them, "Eh, this one needs a squirt of paint! How about it!"

"Let's get in with them, maybe we can get some!"

He grabbed a blue patch by the tail, caught a fist in the face and was slammed against the wall, just brushing Aesh.

The revelers went on yelping, pulling tails, and paying no attention, while the yellow painted player did two cartwheels, tripped over his clogs on the third, was picked up and hauled off.

But the fun-seeker yelled at Aesh, "You hit me!"

Aesh, who had been sidling along the wall toward a doorway, stopped, determined not to *shift* again, and said calmly, "I did not hit you."

Accuser's hand had a knife now, Aesh grabbed at his wrist—

A crack of lightning broke the sky wide open.

Eyes around him staring: "Eh, that's the Emperor!"

*

Those surrounding him disappeared with a hiss of air, except one: the knife-holder.

Aesh stared at him. A memory stirred. *"Not all of us want these damned aliens!" Breaking his staff in two against the railing. "Are there not enough of them eating us up already?"*

That one who had lurched at Genever in the Birthing Center and was stopped by Delius.

Aesh reached the door. The stranger took one step nearer. The rest of the audience had slunk away at the word *Emperor* and the street belonged to the one with the knife.

A powerful voice called, "Aesh-seed, is that you?"

The stranger was gone.

Aesh was through the door, looking down the long dim-lit hall lined with wheeled baskets, while the night shift that followed in took no notice of him.

He knew where he was. Where his unconscious had brought him. Just inside the doorway he leaned against the dirty brick wall to take breath, feeling the oily sweat dripping from his webbed armpits.

Down the hallway and around the corner were his three siblings. This was not one of the compounds men visited for sexual pleasure or in the hope of begetting males. Attendants and visitors came only to clean and feed these sterile ones, scrub floors and carry away the leavings.

The dark cloaked figure confronted him: "Aesh?"

Aesh found his breath. "Ohr-father?" He knew that Ohr paid for the care of the siblings, to keep them in the city instead of the outreaches where they were often left to lie unclean and unfed until they died; and also that he visited at night, in shame, as so many others did. Emperors did not come here at all.

"You here? And naked? Were you with those painted rousters?"

"I was doing my best not to be," Aesh said, a bit sharply. "I was on my bed at home when I … *shifted.*"

"Eh. You were troubled."

"Yesterday my friend, Dos Ramos that you met, was killed. My guard wounded." The weight of sorrow hit his shoulders.

"And you, were you hurt?"

"No. Those ones haven't tried to kill me yet. Whoever they are … One of them out here…"

"Who?"

Who was the knife meant for? How could he know I'd be here? "Nothing. I said nothing."

"Take my cloak and staff. Aesh-seed, you have a stranger's eyes. Come home with me tonight."

"Ohr-father, I'm still the Emperor no matter how I look now, and much as I want to, I cannot run home like a little child."

"Then let me take you back to your court, I have a wagon out back, with Har."

"I will visit these with you first."

And looking down at his eyeless siblings diapered and stinking in their baskets, wordless mouths snorting, limbs twitching unconsciously, he could remember his young self, doing conscript service in these halls, bitterly wishing his father's position as a civic leader did not keep him from being a dirtweed smoker, a painted tumbler, any dirty thing to mask the nausea.

Now Ohr did the cleansing, and would not let him share it.

Every day all of these strange "people" were forced to arrange themselves in long lines and say "Yes sir" and raise their hands to their faces, if they had hands or faces. The red beast, Rrengha, did not exactly have either; she went her own way and no one stopped her: likely everyone was as frightened of her as Ruah had been, but now was afraid no longer. But she dared not ask the question: *Why do* you *stay here in this ugly place?* Perhaps the answer was the same as her own: for food.

"What are the people doing all these things for?" she asked.

"They are getting ready to fight over who owns the great wealth of the world," Rrengha said. "I think it is not so great as they expect."

"This world?" Thinking of the vast ship that had brought her and the others, the great curve of the planet below.

"Any world that is not as strong as they."

"I am here because I was starving. I don't think I would be much of a fighter."

"All the more reason to eat up and watch out."

She dared to ask: "Why are you here, then?"

"My people send me here to find the ancient history of my world. Here they tell me the history is all preserved on Fthel Five, not Four, but nobody gives me a way to go there. I also want food, and I want to go back to my world Ungruarkh."

More than ever did Ruah dream of home.

A FATE PORTENDED

Clearing brush, eating tasteless food, falling into tormented sleep, she lost count of days. Perhaps there were no more than three or four, five at the most. Imprisoned once more, as she had been in the ship that brought her, the hospital that tested her, the laboratory that exploded and sent her into the wilderness. And her body did not fit anyone else's idea of a human being. Not here.

And the attacks … the child at the hospital park, that was one who had not been taught better and needed a good nip on the ear; the stinking tramps knew better but were nearer to animals; the clean one with the weapon did not mean to kill her: she knew that his stungun was the same kind that the Observers at home on Barrazan V used on wild animals. That one wanted to put her to sleep and—what then?

There were those here who reminded her of him—the ones called Earthers—and she stayed well away from most of them.

Her tent-mate, the red beast called Rrengha, was often restless; at night she would rouse herself to wander in the darkness and her thoughts were closed. Then Ruah was so bitterly lonely that even her dreams were bitter, for in them she was at home on Barrazan V and her family group had forgotten her, and drawn together to leave no room for her.

One more new day much like yesterday: spent clearing brush, eating some kind of nameless mash in the big tent that was made of the same stiff crackling stuff used for nearly all the structures and fabrics here … afternoon rains had come early today or she would have eaten outdoors…

…raising her head from her bowl now, she sensed one of *them* close to her, his thick disgusting body of raw flesh, and one particular smell of sweat. She recognized it. White eyes and square yellow teeth, snarling.

Stungun. Shift and shift again—

He had none of those weapons here, he was wearing ragged clothes, with nothing but a water bottle hanging from his belt. He muttered something to another of his kind, rose to toss his bowl into the washwagon then squatted again, balanced to rise, keeping his eyes on her. Curling black hair burst from the neck of his shirt and he scratched in it with rasping nails.

Even though he had no weapon the fear hit her like a knife in her breastbone. Trying to seem calm, she glanced about for Grushka with the tick-tock arm and did not see her; fear rose like a weapon from her breastbone to her brain and she gulped the last swallow of her food, jumped up and ran though there was nowhere to run, and the sparking fence was the limit of every direction.

Somewhere in back of her one of the usual fights broke out with shouts and cracking punches, but she ran through the rain and did not stop or look back, only heard the thud and splash of the boots on the wet clay soil coming after her.

He yelled, "Thought you'd got away, lady-dog?" She realized that he was only following her at her own pace, sure of his catch because there was nowhere else for her to go, but her terror would not let her stop; the fence was here now, only three spans away with its twined wires and sharp spikes and finally with desperate fury, rather than give in she launched her body against

*

the air and realized that instinct would never let her destroy herself, not in that way. And saw in one instant of horror that there was one more of those brutes waiting—

—to grab with arms like bands of iron, then a deep sting that made her bite her tongue with its pain, and the words that echoed in her head before the silence and darkness:

It worked! You could of got skinned if—

I know these kind even better than you do. Just don't you fuck it up now, make sure the old bastard pays—

᠃

She became aware. A hand was pulling her tail … not pulling. Caressing. She shuddered, and did not want to open her eyes.

"I won't hurt you," the voice said, in her own language.

Through slitted eyelids she saw a squat old Earther with a snub nose and a white pointed beard. His white suit had iridescent buttons on it; he was crouched on a great chair that looked like a golden throne from old legends, and holding a glass that had a stem, and red liquid in it. She was lying on a fabric floor covering that was thick and soft, with woven patterns of unreal leaves and flowers the color of the liquid in the glass.

I know you will not hurt me, she did not say, with the comforting sense of her fangs catching her lower lip.

He sipped from the glass, and someone else's loud voice said, "You satisfied, Mister Vanbrennan? Not a scratch on her."

She knew who that was, and did not turn to look. Her eyelids were still heavy from whatever poison had stupefied her. She began to pull herself up slowly and no one stopped her.

The old man said to that voice's owner, "You will be paid," and to Ruah, "You may move as much as you like, but you will not *shift* because the drug you have been given prevents it."

She stood and did not care for being unclothed in this fearful presence. "You are keeping me here forever…" Half a question; her voice was hoarse and cracked. She rubbed her arms to smooth the guardhairs down.

The room was vast and there were hangings of woven stuff on the walls. Windows of many shapes had colored transparent panes set into them, and there were a half score of other chairs, as well as benches and tables, all with twisted legs and bearing strange objects just as twisted.

From the way that all these ornaments, rippling draperies, lamplights, sunbeams through glass stained red, green, yellow, purple, all among bright reflecting mirrors, were swarming around her, she began to feel half dizzy, almost as if she might be on her home world in the midst of its storms and thrashing branches.

The old man widened his lips in what he might consider a smile, and answered, "Forever is not quite the length of a lifetime."

At that moment an old serving woman dressed in a black coverall offered her a leather tunic, saying, "This is for you, Ruah, put it on."

She had nothing to gain by refusing, and while she was turning her head to work it through the neck band, glimpsed, and then stared across the vast room to its farthest corner. There too among all other ornaments was one more raised lamp, and below it on a slanting framework, what looked at first like an altar to old gods: a wooden container decorated with carvings like the vines and leaves she knew on her world, that once in the far past might have been filled with offerings but now under its glass cover held the dead body of a very old Meshar woman with grey-flecked fur and white guardhairs.

She pulled down the tunic slowly; it had a slit to accommodate her tail. That much freedom at least, she had.

"She is dead, that one," she said.

"Yes. That was the forever she was given. You are taking her place now."

DELIUS AND NATALYA

Morning: Delius locked himself again into his cell of the hive, left all of his machines shut down, and tried once more to put pieces together. He thought of darkening the glassy walls, and realized that the over-dramatic gesture would reinforce his sense of imprisonment.

He had spent a lifetime following orders, most of which had gone against his grain, driving populations from their worlds and stirring rage among them, making promises and dodging death to keep them, finding the merest of rewards in saving thousands of lives. Compelled to leave his wife and son to live without him. How alone Zakarian had been, how bitterly lonely Aesh Seven must be.

And how bitterly I am. The one friend, gone; and that friendship no more than a knife's edge.

His wrist comm chimed, and he sighed. *At least I haven't had time to sink completely into self-pity … thank God for that.*

Mbai was waiting for him with her elbows on her console and her hands clasped.

"Sit down, Delius. I want to apologize."

"For what?"

"For letting Genever rile me over those damned transcripts from the pact with Aesh Seven. You may be angry with Semdah's esping you, and legally you're right, but it showed us once and for all that you couldn't avoid making that promise to Aesh."

Delius smiled wearily. "I'm not likely to bring any action on that account. But I do want a favor."

"If I can manage it."

"To leave off finishing those reports of the same facts that have already been made by all the members of the expedition, and spend the rest of my time here with my wife and son."

"You can have that."

"Good. Thank you." He stood up. And as an afterthought, said, "Have you heard anything of that Meshar woman you've been looking for?"

"Yes, we've been trying to trace her by her chip. But every time we locate her she *shifts* and disappears before we can send anyone after her." There was an odd look on her face, as if there was something important that she did not want to say. "A strange thing happened today … her signal has disappeared."

"Where was she?" He half expected Mbai to tell him to mind his own business.

But she said, "It's more than strange. She somehow got collected into a criminal group that was planning an outworld raid, but there's a police action taking care of them, and there's no way we could interfere with that without getting all of the media sucking at us—and of course while we were working at that she *shifted* again and…" She moistened her lips.

"Turned up again. Somewhere in the Fire Trees sector and before we could think of doing anything she blinked out."

Set up an estate for her on a piece of land he owns down south in the Fire Trees sector, says Zakarian.

Delius found himself standing with his mouth open for a second, and said, "It doesn't mean for sure she's with old Vanbrennan."

"No. It means we have no signal. Just forget we had this conversation, Delius."

One of the things Zakarian knew…

❧❧

Out of there then, alone this time, the kid in school, and pacing the moving walkway with its creaks and shadows, and eerie blinking lights. Several of the check-in points had been eliminated. Their absence gave a sense of: nothing much more to stave off here, the damage is done.

But sight of Natalya, ah, was a different matter. She was off the bed, and resting in a padded chair, her black hair braided by some kind nurse to hide the wound; wearing a white nightsuit, no more sludgy greens. And she was smiling.

Delius fell to his knees before her and laid his head on her thighs. "Say the word," he whispered.

"Not quite ready yet." She was laughing. "Before you"—a catch of breath—"before you leave here…"

"I'll wait."

As he rose to his feet, he saw Horrocks at the door, with a fist raised to knock. Delius flushed, and Natalya laughed again. But Delius was not embarrassed to be caught looking foolish; he dreaded looking Horrocks in the face after what Mbai had told him, and trying to think what to say that would not show he knew, and he could not keep from wondering what Horrocks knew: he was afraid for him.

He opened the door, but Horrocks only smiled in his painful way and said, "I'm so glad to see Natya looking better."

"I couldn't agree more," Delius said.

* * N I N E * *

CAPITAL CITY EQUATORIAL LANDS

Ohr left Aesh Seven at the lane leading to the back gate, saying, "Aesh-seed, I and Har will stay alongside you the night if that will help you sleep easier."

"The safer you are in your own house the easier I will sleep," Aesh said. "Hire another guard—two more guards—and take some of the weight off Har." He said this in a low voice so as not to offend Har; on the way home, still half-stunned from that *shift,* that knife, he had begun to think more deeply of what was happening around him. A killer aiming at the child Shemesh, the murder of Dos Ramos, the "rouster" with the knife. *Perhaps that one happened to be in that street, was not sent to kill me … or my father. But … I believe that they—and who are 'they'?—want to isolate me. And so they have done…*

The guard at the gate was startled to see him, but said nothing, and he was glad of that, and also that the Chief of Guards was not there to annoy him.

He had a few hours of furiously dreaming sleep, and was glad for that much.

As the Council gathered Aesh found two thirds of its members putting their fists to their mouths and their elbows pointing at him: not a good sign. No new alien representative had yet been sent from orbit on this day, and Aesh found no one to ease the atmosphere; he wondered if after the murder of Dos Ramos, the company officials had become too fearful. He did not sit down.

Surprisingly, it was Arvig's son Ayin who began the attack:

"Aesh-lord, last night you were seen behaving very strangely in disgusting circumstances. Do you have an explanation for this?"

His tone was courteous enough, and Aesh answered in the same manner: "That was an event that happened beyond my control and I—"

Givor broke in: "That is not an explanation!"

"First tell me: how did you know I was in disgusting circumstances? Who was watching, Councillor? Do you have agents to track my *shifting*? Or perhaps you were spying on my father? You have agents, do you not? One with a knife?"

Givor said harshly, "You still have not answered the question."

"What can I say except that I *shifted* against my will as everyone may do in fear or sorrow, and found myself in those disgusting circumstances without clogs or tunic, feeling very foolish. You let all of those stunned and drunken fellows run free, even though your watchman was there to judge me. A guard without identification! Why did you not stop that one with his knife pointing at me? Ring the alarm bells? The same thing happened half a tenday ago when I heard all of the rioting in the street, when the same sort were taking babies from the Mother-Halls and tossing them in the air. Where were the guards then?"

"That is not what we have been discussing."

"I beg pardon! What then? What am I accused of?"

Givor was visibly listing the charges in his mind.

"Deluding our people with impossible promises, taking the child, putting him into danger, bringing even more meddling aliens down on our heads!" He paused for breath, panting. "Why should we care about your dream of women? The Angry-God has cursed you with sterility and sterile siblings! Isn't that a sign of the gods' contempt for what you want?"

Aesh's guardhairs rose at the insult, but he said levelly, "It is the gods up here in the sky above our heads that have contempt for what we want! No matter whether or not we create whole women, we will always have such gods as long as there is anything valuable on this world.

"Those companies prefer the Shar as we are—incomplete! Choking in the air we can hardly breathe, that they promised to clean and only make worse with their mines and machines! You believe we are being treated so well, you are happy to take the bits of metal the aliens give us to pay for the wealth of our world, for us to exchange them to buy food and clothing, when what we need is to be taught to make and grow our own.

"The more time we take caring for females who ought to be able to care for themselves—and our children—the less trouble we cause the 'benefactors'. All of this government is a sham, and I am the sham Emperor!"

"Enough! Enough!" From some fold in his robe, Givor's hand found a bright-bladed knife and plunged it into the Council table.

The Council members gasped and shrank back. The Chief of Guards, who had been at the door, stepped in quickly; after a moment of shocked silence he moved away.

Aesh said, "Yes, that is enough. I apologize for speaking the truth so bluntly." He looked around at the lot of them, then for a moment stared at the knife in the table, his mind flickering from the deeply burled wood, to the frieze on his wall. "So, all of you Councillors, is there anyone here who is for me?"

Arvig said, "I have always stood at your side, Aesh- lord, and I rebuke my son."

But there were only a half-score of others, who raised their hands slowly, and Aesh nodded at them. "I'm pleased to have your trust, Arvig, and also for you few who are not quite enough." He pulled the gold clasp from his shoulder and placed it on the table next to the knife, then tied the shoulder strap into an awkward knot and picked up his staff. He said, "You will of course want the agreement of our alien advisors in their wisdom, and when that comes I will be out of your tower." And added, "If anyone dares to harm that child, the father of mothers, he will answer to me."

He stepped around his circle of Councillors and out of the door. He still could hear Givor's stern voice: "Archivist, will you record this abdication?" And the Archivist's whimpering assent.

⸎

The Chief of Guards was leaning on his staff, regarding him.

Aesh looked back with a curl of his lip. "Ah-yah! I have had my thumbs twisted as much as you might want, Chief of Guards!"

"It seems so far I am the only one who has not asked for that." The Chief of Guards snorted, "But that Givor, you know, he'll never be named Emperor. And if I'm wrong and it turns out that he is, he won't last long. He's shown too much of himself today."

"That's not my affair any longer. I'll be away from here soon."

"Life will be duller."

"Not for me." Aesh drew up his shoulders with a shiver, chilled in spite of the heat of noon.

"Here's Sefer," the Chief of Guards said. "Somewhat badly used, but still walking."

Sefer came running. He had a shaven patch and bandage above one eye, but was otherwise his hearty self. "Aesh-lord! Tell me I am still your guard!"

"I am no longer your lord, Sefer, and I give you your freedom, at least from my hire. Our rulers have decided that I am not one of them, and you will have a new emperor."

Sefer cried, "Chief of Guards, say that's not so!"

The Chief of Guards stuck out a lower lip in something like regret. "I'm afraid it is, young one."

Aesh drew Sefer aside, and said in a low voice, "Sefer, I am afraid for my life and yours as well, and I think you ought to find a person, a place, anything that will be less dangerous for you."

"No! I will go if you don't believe I have served you well, but not otherwise."

"This is no story of great deeds told to children that we are going through—"

Sefer spoke more words than he had ever done in one speech: "Aesh-lord, I'm afraid that you are in much more danger now from all of them that never wanted real women. News runs fast and you need whatever help you can find. I don't mean danger from someone like Givor. Givor's an honest man. Cruel and wrongheaded but honest. Just the same, Aesh-lord, I cannot work for Givor or any of the ones around him! I will follow wherever you go."

Aesh shook his head wearily. "The pickings will be small. And I am not your lord."

"The cheapest slice of meat and a boiled tebbek root will more than fill my belly."

And I cannot promise even that. But I need … anyone.

"If you come with me, then, you take your chances."

"I will."

꙰꙰

The last evening in the tower.

Aesh undid the clumsy knot of his shoulder strap and replaced it with the worn bronze clasp the old local priest had given him at his manhood ceremony, folded the leather tunic and laid out one of the old coarse-woven fabric ones he had brought to this tower eight years ago: in its pocket was the same handful of coins he had earned working for his father after his duty in the Mother-Halls. From a shelf, he pulled down the pleated Emperor's Cloak that was supposed to give him dignity but only tangled around his ankles; it would be good enough to sleep on if there was nothing else. Everything else he used belonged to the Equatorial Lands.

He took his dinner in the courtyard for the last time and the guards greeted and served him with the usual courtesy. He was content not to have their farewells or any sign that might put them out of favor with the new emperor.

Upstairs again he looked out of the window for the night view. The barely cooling wind had cleared the sky for a few moments, and a star became visible beyond the orbiters, the world's gods. Down below in the courtyard the guards, freed from imperial duty, were engaged in pebble-tossing games, mock fights, cartwheels … lives easier than tending the unwomen.

One of the pairs of mock-fighters eased their knuckle-bruising into slaps that gradually became caresses, then, clinging together moved into a shadowed corner and wrapped arms and tails into a tight clasp, grunting and plunging.

The others in the courtyard gathered to watch them, and began tapping their staffs on the stones in applause. The Chief of Guards ran forward, snarling and shaking his staff. No one seemed to hear him; he stopped, watched for a few moments and turned away.

Aesh also turned away, thinking how he had wished in his youth to be one of those street-running "rousters," and wondering if it might not have been so bad—and a lot cleaner—to be a guard.

He laid down on his bedding and somehow slept with no worse dreams than usual.

Departure was simple: Aesh woke, washed, and dressed in his old woven tunic. He gathered his belongings without taking one more glance at the frieze of joyful women with their children, or touching the stone seal with its jewel stars. Shemesh would not come here again to play with that, the whole world in his hands.

Aesh went downstairs and found Sefer sleeping on a mat he had spread out inside the entrance to the tower.

"It's time, Sefer," he said.

Sefer rose immediately, shaking the sleep from his head. "Where are we to go, then?"

"I have nowhere else to go but to my father's house, the shortest way we can find, and after that we must think of what to do."

In the courtyard a sleepy guard offered breakfast.

Aesh tilted his head in gratitude. "Eat well," he told Sefer, "and so will I."

The sun burned down on their heads and shoulders, and when a guard spilled a few drops of his mullendew tea, the flagstones hissed and steamed. The heat had often bothered Aesh: but it was part of his home's surroundings; at this moment, watching the drift of vapor on hot stone, he began to find it truly oppressive.

With a last look around the courtyard he could see no one to wish him well and no reason to linger. "A lot of cowards," Sefer muttered.

"No. I insulted them. Truth is often insulting."

"Look, here is Arvig," Sefer said. "What does he want?"

Aesh said nothing. He was sure that he knew.

Arvig came slowly, and put his hand on Aesh's shoulder. He mumbled, "The representative from Xanthrotek, speaking for all others in their orbit of our world, has agreed with … the Council's decision."

"I expected so," Aesh said, and Arvig turned away.

The Chief of Guards came over, saying, "Let me open the gate for you. I'm not afraid to wish you well."

"Good," Aesh said. "Take care of the new Emperor."

"I will. Eh, I will!"

⁊⍧

"What way are we going, Aesh-lord?"

"The shortest, across the road and down the alley behind the Mother-Halls—"

"I know that one, where they take the trash out in the morning and after dinner."

"And it's not very clean but it should be quiet."

Sefer said doubtfully, "At midnight it's quiet. After the morning meal…"

"I don't know any other way where it's quiet, or anywhere else to go." The friends he had believed in were nowhere.

"I said I'd follow you."

"Ayeh, and it's too hot for standing still. Come, then."

⁊⍧

The lane was dim and narrow, lined with public latrines and equally stinking garbage troughs where small animals burrowed, invisible beneath the trash. Clouds of insects flickered above them. The walls were shored with flaking plaster; they and the cobbles here were nearly as hot as the ones under the sun.

Aesh and Sefer took quick, quiet steps. The windows had no panes, and Aesh could hear barrows rattling down the halls inside. He hoped that they were empty.

He kept his eyes ahead to avoid looking at the graffiti, crude muddy scrawls of insults and depictions of women, or what men thought women looked like.

A head appeared at one of the windows.

"Look! Look!" Eyes glaring and pointing fingers.

"That's a stranger."

"No, it's not!"

"Who is it, then?

"That's the Emperor—the one that got pushed out!"

"The one that loves the women so much!"

"Let's take a look!"

Aesh moved faster, but four or five of the workers barreled out of there, from doors before and behind him. They grinned and bared their fangs.

He snarled at them, "What do you want!" But they paid no mind.

"Is this one truly the Emperor?"

"He was. He sounds like one."

"He's wearing rags now, he's no more than a beggar."

"Do whatever we like with a beggar!"

"Kick him, jump him, roll him in mud—"

Their bodies began to nudge him, elbows pushing back and forth; he raised a hand against Sefer's growling fury and pushed back whatever arms he could not dodge, trying not to fall on the sludgy cobbles. He did not want to use his staff and start a real riot.

Behind him a voice shrilled, "Emperor of women! Where are you now?" They closed in, hands clutched at him, other voices joined in screeching, one pair of hands grabbed him around the neck, one more dragged at his tail, jerked it up, still another pair reached under his tunic, a hand pushed between his legs, claws grasping for his sperm sac and—

Aesh howled with shock and fury and struck out hard, but all of the arms let go abruptly because Sefer, caring nothing about riots, was thrashing the attackers with his staff and howling even louder.

"Stop, Sefer, stop!"

Two of the attackers were by now lying curled up on the cobbles, begging for their lives, and the rest had *shifted*, but Sefer kept at it. "I want to kill them!"

Aesh, panting with both fear and anger, forced words through his teeth: "If I were still Emperor I might let you, but I am not. Those poor fools, they were playing with us—guards will run to kill us now when they see them bloody! Come away from here!"

No *shift* ever happens when it's needed.

And bad news travels fast. Eh, a pity I don't believe in Angry-God, for he surely believes in me.

He limped away, sore from bruises and scratches, and no one followed but Sefer, out of there and into the cleaner sunlight.

"They were doing their best to hurt you," Sefer said. "I should have seen that coming."

Aesh paused to brush dead insects out of his fur. "More likely you saved my skin. Tell me, Sefer, where did you learn to fight like that?"

"My father served as a guard in the Polar Monarchy. He taught me."

"He surely did. Let's move along now. I chose the wrong hole to hide in. Eh, that's some kind of start to a new life."

FTHEL IV: GALACTIC FEDERATION:
DELIUS AND NATALYA AND HORROCKS

Delius was packing. Hot weather wear, plus the usual getup expected for an Envoy: dark blue with gold braid. Nose filters. Oxycaps. Plus the appointment to have the oxycap socket reinstalled—a painful process attached to outworld voyages.

But he felt a stir of guilt at what he would rarely admit to himself: that the beginning of a new venture to a strange world stimulated him to a point of intoxication, at least for the short while until he sank into cold-sleep, and woke to the suspicious glares of the colonists he would be obliged to force out of their homes, their communities. Their lives.

Here there was a difference. His mission was one degree more sophisticated: drawing a troubled people out of their ignorance and suspicion. Hoping he was capable of that.

૪૪

That evening after wringing permission from her doctor, Natalya rose from her crumpled bed and after some practice walked with Delius and the boy to their lodgings, the nearest to a home that they could make, in the service of Galactic Federation.

James clung to her hand for dear life all the way and would let go only when he was assured that she would stay the night.

When he was asleep Delius and Natalya settled themselves in what passed for a sitting room and he poured them both a share of the whiskey an acquaintance had stolen out of a diplomat's cabinet.

Natalya shivered with pleasure. "I was so tired of that glass box. I was getting worn out by Horrocks too, but I'll have to work with him if we ever get back to work."

"Is he falling for you, Natya? I don't blame him, but he'd better not!"

"No," she said quietly. "He tells me things I'd rather not hear."

Delius waited a moment before answering: "Let me guess … about his father?"

"Painful … I tell him he doesn't need to tell me such private things, but he can't bear to tell anyone else, and he really needs to share the burden."

Delius said carefully, "Did he say anything about the Meshar woman that's gone missing?"

"No … Meshar are a sore point with him. But," she whispered, "what he did tell me, his father won't see him. When he tries to visit, it's in that big estate down south, the servants won't let him in, and he says one time he heard his father yelling, 'Keep that bastard out of here!' Do you think he's telling the truth?"

"Yes, that sounds like the truth from Horrocks. But I don't know whether he's is really the old man's son or not. Zakarian did a lot of muttering about that before he got himself blown up."

"But he did all that good work on those worlds of Oerstmann and Pembo, and it was his father that sent him out to do it!" She shook her head. "He's such a good person, I can't just tell him to shut up."

"Do you believe your crew will really be able to finish that work?"

"Reconstruction of the center hasn't begun, and the crew are so demoralized they don't care. All that work normalizing the sperm and ova—what we think, hope, is normal, based on getting rid of one counterclockwise twist in a chromosome. But we needed that beginning that got blown up, and even if it went perfectly it would take a hundred years just to—oh, I don't want to talk about it!"

"Don't, then. We'll talk of something else … we don't even need to talk." He slid open his zippers and shrugged out of the murky green cloth with its imitation gold knobs, and gently released Natalya from her frosty whites.

Then they were alone, flesh to flesh in the darkness

LEAVING HOME

Delius had lingered to say painful goodbyes filled with false cheerfulness to Natya and James, and now was trudging down the last length of cheap carpet in the Terrarium. His oxycap socket hurt, and various parts of his body stung with the injections of seventy-odd drugs to keep him alive on Shar. Two of the rugged crew he had worked with on the first expedition were waiting on the buzzer pad, along with Kohav, who was burning to go home.

His baggage was in the port being loaded in the shuttle but he was lugging an orbispex loaded with a thousand instructive documents and vast scenes of the world and its inhabitants gathered by survey and satellite. He had no more to do now than get a last word from Rosa Mbai. As he was passing the doorway to one of the smaller meeting rooms, he saw something that made him slow his pace.

The remaining Shar who had come with Kohav was there, speaking with a young Meshar woman named Levona; after all the long years of separation they spoke different languages, but in hesitant phrases of *lingua* he was telling her about Kohav's son Shemesh, who was going to be the Father of Mothers.

Delius went by silently, not to break the mood.

Maybe. Just maybe.

ᔐᔍ

Mbai met him in one of the interview rooms, two chairs and a desk. She had creases under her eyes, and bracket lines from nose to mouth.

"I wish you well. I always have. You know that."

"Thank you, I do know that. But something's wrong—what is it?"

She sighed. "Our informant on Shar tells us that our golden boy, Aesh, has been kicked out. That's no surprise. He's too honorable and passionate about Restoration for them. But they need him. I only hope you can find him. That's why we're sending you there. But the other news is much worse, and may wreck everything. One of those mutants has been born to a Meshar woman on Barrazan Five."

And maybe not.

"Eh, that's all they need to add to those handless stumps. What are they doing about it out there?"

He did not dare ask her about Horrocks, his father and the fate of the woman Ruah.

"Nothing. It died soon after birth, thank God."

Or whoever helped it along. He knew those Meshar. "They'll have to take that mother out of the breeding stock…"

"Yes. They don't have all that many. You do what you can for the Shar, Delius, you've been in the business long enough."

～ ҡ

His crew, Mick and Jacko, looked the same as ever, bristle-headed standard issue for big blond Mick, Jacko dark and intense. Cobb, a stranger, was not really a member of the crew, but a new man brought in by Semdah, a biologist; he had red hair rapidly whitening, bursting red brows and permanently flushed cheeks. Delius would have preferred to include a woman but Upstairs worried about intruding with female hormones, no matter how alien.

Crammed in his slot to wait out the orbit, and the last coldsleep injection, he pulled the orbispex from his zip to scroll the instructions that the vastness of GalFed had loaded for him.

The document that caught his eye was a survey of the world Shar that showed again how steadily the population was declining, and the quickening rate of its decrease. It was no wonder: only the ones with the fiercest passion for children would go into the dark halls where the monsters waited.

As Delius fell into coldsleep he had a flash dream that the true-form Meshar females were an aberration and Angry-God had created the Shar to mate with unwomen.

* * T E N * *

NO EMPEROR

The rest of the way to Ohr's house was along streets of breath-holding silence, so it seemed to Aesh.

"Everyone here has gone to work," Sefer said. "I wish those ones that were so happy pulling our tails were busier."

"So do I," Aesh said. "If only this world was." He stopped on the word.

"What were you wanting to say, Aesh-lord?"

"What I've said too many times already. Less angry, I suppose. It surely is very quiet."

"Sleeping quiet, frightening quiet or dangerous quiet, do you think?"

"I didn't know there were so many kinds. My father's house is over there, and nobody's about. Hey-yey! Har, Ohr-father!"

The door slammed open, an unknown voice cried, "Who's there!"

"Aesh, the son of my father Ohr!" Aesh called. "Who are you?"

A person he had never seen came out and stepped down. He had long fangs and held a crossbow; the sight of it gave Aesh an involuntary shiver, though he had been well trained in its use.

"I am his new guard," the stranger said. He was tall, and bent slightly to peer at Aesh. "Ayeh, I know you! You are the Emperor!"

"Not any longer."

"You are my Emperor," the guard said.

"Then you are a friend."

"Your father has gone into that place across the road, into those ruins, I don't know why, but he will be here soon."

A voice called from back of them, "I am here."

Aesh turned and found his father standing in an opening between two walls of the great ruins across the road. "Ohr-father?"

Ohr came forward, and Har came after him out of the ruins. "Eh, what has happened to you, Aesh?"

Aesh had forgotten that his fur had collected filth from the alley he was tumbling in. "I came a short way that was longer than I expected."

Ohr surveyed him, and half-whispered, "You were an Emperor and now you are a beggar."

Aesh said quietly, "Do you really believe that?"

"Aesh-seed, the things you work for are fine and good, but the things you do are so foolish. Already the news has come that you rebuked everyone on the Council."

"Father, you did more good for this city than I could ever do for the country. It was a cleaner and more peaceful city when you helped run it, and that was because you were not in the way of the aliens, they left you alone and you were free to do the work. I'm not greedy for power, but the Emperor is something made of sticks to frighten children, a creature of the aliens. Tell me, has someone attacked you?"

"Why do you ask? There are plenty running about and screaming insults, but no one from this area."

"You were in the ruins. I thought you might be taking shelter."

"Hiding, you mean," Ohr said evenly. "No. That may happen, but I have not made plans yet. Ai, Aesh-seed, where are all those in this world who want to have true women? Are any of these aliens really working for us as they claim?"

Wearily, Aesh said, "I can't tell any longer. I hope there are. Is there a place in those ruins where Sefer and I might sleep tonight? I don't want to put you at risk."

Ohr stood looking into Aesh's eyes long and carefully. "You will sleep in my house, and three guards will protect you inside it—you as well, Sefer."

"Pardon, Ohr-father, I was only afraid for you."

"I didn't go there to hide. Let me wash that filth off you and I'll tell you … no, after our meal, I'll show you."

"I will clean him!" Sefer cried.

Ohr said, "You? You have enough dirt of your own."

꙳꙳

Ohr insisted on leaving Sefer at the house with his new guard, and, having fetched a lamp, he and Har led Aesh into the ruins. The jagged walls glowed dimly in the deep red sky of coming rain. Paths of broken stone blocks led into the openings of the walls, and there were fillings of round pebbles between them, and long leafless vines forcing their yellow growing tips among those.

No one knew who had built this structure; it was ancient and in ruins when the Shar population expanded far enough to find it, and there were stories of great civilizations who had come before, who had moved away or else foundered and died.

The openings led into more shattered walls, more paths of blocks and pebbles crusted with rotting fungus. In some of the corners were scatterings of bones left by unknown creatures of ancient times; other walls were broken through by the dead branches of trees whose lifelines were exhausted.

Aesh, trying to keep balance in all those passageways, followed Ohr and Har with growing unease, starting to wonder if his father, a tower of rationality, was beginning to crumble like this building.

Ohr stopped at an opening where three deep steps led into darkness, and Har lit the lamp and stepped down. Ohr followed, and then Aesh. The room they entered was barely lit by a small electric lamp, and the air was cool here, almost cold.

The place was scrubbed clean. There was a table, to hold the lamp, a water jug, some packets of food; a stool, to support a very old man, so old that he seemed covered in frost; a mat, lined in clean cloths, to hold the unwoman wrapped in a diaper.

She was breathing, trembling once in a while so that her whitened guardhairs quivered. One of her arms had been broken when she was young, and left unset so that it healed twisted.

Long ago Ohr had told Aesh of an ancestor in the time when women were whole, a powerful priestess who had borne one of the earliest of the mutants, and killed herself for the shame of it. He did not know if the story was true, but could not help thinking of it as he watched the shivering creature taking rough breath.

Ohr gestured at the old man: "I feed him, he feeds her," he murmured. "I knew her. I found her again last year when she was being sent to the inland halls to die. Should we not be allowed to love even one of these? It is forbidden to do that, waste food and care on them. I am committing a crime."

Har snorted so loudly that the old man startled and nearly fell off the stool. "He's always saying that! Don't listen." He lifted the lantern. "Time to go."

Aesh did not say a word. He looked sadly at Ohr.

One of our mothers? If she could speak to you, what would both of you say about having four sterile descendants?

The rain began to patter down the walls.

He slept that one night in his father's house. He had not slept along with others in many years, and their breaths were like the rain, comforting.

ツ℞

For lack of enough benches Sefer and the new guard, Bosor, ate the morning meal as they had done on the evening before, squatting on the stone floor. Afterward, Aesh gathered his bit of baggage and picked up his staff.

Ohr cried, "What! You're leaving now?"

"I came only to tell you what happened and make sure you were safe. I'm not staying here to eat your food and crowd your house." He went outside and stood on the step.

Ohr followed. "Where will you go, then?"

"To the Western Islands or the Polar Monarchy to look for work. In the Mother-Halls if need be. I've done that before."

Ohr was looking at him intently. "Are you angry at yourself, Aesh-seed?"

"I was accused of crimes that never existed, being in places I never meant to go, caring too much for the child Shemesh—I may be angry, Ohr-father, but not at myself."

"And you will swallow all of this and hide away?"

"I won't go begging to the Council, I won't lick the feet of the aliens. You were right to tell me not to, you were also right that time when you said that everything had fallen apart. I made foolish mistakes, putting the child in danger when I was trying to save him and—"

"Enough, enough! Today it's you that's saying too much. If you stay here, I'll find work or you, I know the people."

Aesh said, "It's not right to stay … I was glad to work with you when I was younger, but I can't care much for myself if I feed off you." *And where can I go and live in peace?*

Ohr said, "On the second corner of Island Road there is an eating place that takes lodgers. I've lived there myself. I will lend you a little money, and you will pay me back when you find work."

Aesh swallowed hard and said, "That's good of you, Ohr-father, and I'll go to the lodging, but I have enough money for now." He picked up his staff. "Come, Sefer!"

He had not gone more than three or four steps down the road when men began coming out of their houses. At first he thought they were on their way to work, but they were coming toward him, tapping their staffs, not in a hurry.

Aesh slowed his steps as well, and then stood leaning on his own staff, with Sefer at his elbow. Something new.

There was nothing unusual about them, people who went to work and walked in the streets.

One of them called, "You were the Emperor!"

"I was."

Sefer began to draw lightning bolts on the gravel with his staff, restlessly. Aesh raised his hand slightly.

The voice rose: "You made all the promises, and what will happen now?"

And another, brandishing his staff, voice rising to a howl in a mix of angry voices: "All these years you made promises and nothing happened! We still have to get our children out of the dead meat we call women, and half what we get is more dead meat that we still have to feed and clean the shit off! What have you got to say to that!"

He nearly said: *Yesterday I was set on by a pack of angry fools who thought it was a sin to want women—do you want to beat me too for not being able to make them? This is like a game of bullies—you get your tail twisted no matter what choice you make!*

But his first aim was to move them away from the ruins where the unwoman slept, and from his father's house. He took a deep breath and said quietly, "I gave my whole life to this work, but I can't force the aliens to create women, if so many of our people don't want them. Even

Galactic Federation can't do that." *And who of them know how to create women?* "If you want to try you will have to choose a small group and present yourselves to the Council with one voice. And not try to frighten anybody or become angry whatever happens. I learned that from my father when he managed this city and it never failed him. That was a city and this is the world and it might work, but I can't promise."

He waited while they gathered together and muttered over this. Then their spokesman sneered, "That's no kind of answer! We'll let you go now, but you better watch out for all the others that feel the way we do."

The look in Sefer's eye made Aesh turn around; Bosor, the newest guard, was standing in the doorway with crossbow aimed; his father had been well warned already, he thought.

"Your father can take care of himself," Sefer said dryly. *As well as you.* The words were unspoken, but Aesh heard them in his mind.

"They may go off now," Aesh said. "But they're not happy. I hope they don't meet up with that lot we fought our way through yesterday."

"I hope we don't meet them either."

"Sefer, you would do better going back north to be a guard in the Polar Monarchy like your father."

"Would I? Up there we lived in Hearth City, and when my father was too old for the Guard he sold vegetables in a street market. One night someone stabbed him in the back and took his bit of money. I was coming from the Mother Hall to go home with him, and I went after the killer and struck him down. He was the son of the Monarch's brother, they let him do anything he wanted. I ran away without stopping to see if he was dead."

"No one came after you?"

"I don't know! I *shifted* and found myself on a raft going down the Great North River, with just enough in my pocket to pay my way."

"And you were able to hire on as a guard here!"

"Yes … no one knew me. Are you afraid of me now, Aesh-lord?"

"No, Sefer! Whether or not you really killed the Monarch's nephew we haven't heard about it here. And I wouldn't blame you either. But now you have no one, then."

"No … it's good to have a father. It was."

৵ল়

Island Road had nothing to do with the Islands except that it led to the dock where rafts and small boats took off to cross the channels. It was lined with buildings of stone or stucco, mainly markets and storehouses. The workers there generally kept their eyes to themselves, though some stared or muttered to see one like Aesh here.

The lodging Ohr had suggested was cheap and moderately clean. Its host was flustered, caught between the honor of having the former emperor for a customer and the fear of being attacked by his enemies. Aesh did his best to soothe him with the pocketful of coins.

For the first time in an octad of years Aesh found himself with nothing to do—nothing to pretend to do, meetings, consultations, orders to give; with servants and guards to carry them out. Here was only enough room for a small table, two benches and a pair of bed-mats: he began to feel like a prisoner as soon as the door shut on the uneasy host. The sweaty grime-striped walls seemed to press against him.

"I've not even been on this street before." He opened the shutters. "It looks quiet enough now."

"No, no, Aesh-lord. It only looks that way. I've been down there and it's too much like the one we were bogged in yesterday, with all them going around howling. Best not keep the window too far open."

"Then we'll be spending a great lot of time in this dim light before we have food and sleep."

"Eh," Sefer dug in his own pocket and pulled out a handful of what looked like street rubbish. "This is a game of sticks and stones. Sometimes I could find another guard to play it with. Most of those others thought it was for babies, but I still like it." He squatted on the hard clay floor. "Here's your stick. I get first toss and you knock it back."

Aesh humored him and hunkered down to play a long ago childhood game. He thought it unlikely that his father had ever played sticks and stones with old Har.

᠅

But he found himself shivering on his bed at midnight. He was in a strange land: the ordinary life, the daily manhood of his people. Except for Sefer, alone. No servants to do his every wish, none of the scientists, suppliers, Councillors listening at his table.

He heard cries in the street and did not know if he was imagining them. He thought of his enemies: those who hated him for what he wanted to do, and the others who scorned him because he had not been able to do it. *There must be some space between them, somewhere.* He had sent Kohav to be his emissary, and one of those with him had been killed. Would Kohav live to come home and reclaim his son?

He thought of women who didn't exist, and who were alien to him in every way except in what he had seen in the frieze that decorated, that blessed the tower wall. Once he had brought his father to see this, and Ohr had stared, to store the vision in his mind.

No one during Aesh's schooling had mentioned or taught of women, but Ohr had found the ancestral Priestess in the dark, distant places where there were archives and records of what the people of Shar had been when they were whole.

And Ohr could still love the unwoman.

Aesh fell asleep into a fearful dream of rioting in the streets, because of the gaping absence of women, the presence of unwomen, and woke up to the crashing of his door.

FTHEL IV:

RUAH IN THE HOUSE OF HENRIK VANBRENNAN

No, he did not hurt her, except for the one time, when he fastened a gold chain around her neck, and she tried to drag it off. Then he gripped her wrist hard. He did not try to fuck her, or even touch her in a sexual way, except to caress her tail and its arrow tip. Then every hair on her skin and not only guardhairs stood on end.

One of those times he clasped her body between his knees, hands on her shoulders, facing away from him, bending to whisper into her ear, and she shrank and hunched down at the feeling of his breath.

I wanted her, her in the box over there, to bear my child, one who would be part of both of us, I gave my Xanthrotek, that my father made, I gave it to the Galaxy and its people to make her one with me, but they couldn't, wouldn't, didn't, I gave that one who calls himself my son, Derek Vanbrennan, that the mother who bore him swears is my son but is a liar...

She crouched rigidly in silence listening to the voice in her own language, own dialect, her joints hurt, she could not move and thought her bones would crack, the words had no meaning and were madness—

...gave that bastard child to the universe, told him to go learn and do this, never come back unless he could give me that child by that woman, he went out there and did for others and never for me, the same way my father did for his other son, the younger one that he loved better than me, and never did for me, and that other one my brother died in a cloud of fire among the meteorites, and my father's heart broke for that, but not for me ... and out on that world where they have none like you, no women at all, they can want and die and never have you, and be damned to them, and be damned to the one that calls himself my son...

148 / Phyllis Gotlieb

As always when Delius left on his offworld missions Natalya worked her way through one or two days of panic before she could busy herself to fill the particular void in her life, and try to keep James cheerful. All of it was hard work; the scars took long to heal, they pulled and itched, even though surgery had made them almost invisible, and she was as tired of the doctor's soothing remarks as she was of the ointments and unguents he prescribed.

Also, this latest interval was intensified by the wreckage of the vast undertaking she and her department had been engaged in; the Shar Project had become a sort of walled town in the New World Hospital: now its medical and research staffs spent their time sitting in on secret discussions by directors and investigators, hiding from media attention and trying to resolve the lack of evidence. The dispirited Shar and Meshar could give no answers either.

Natalya, Mukherjee and Horrocks, part of a team, supported each other: matching each others' loneliness; Mukherjee missing his wife at home up north in Miramar, and Horrocks…

Horrocks had been away for three days, and came back looking sadder and more confused than ever. "My mother died," he said. That was all.

After a day or two of this emptiness, Natalya found herself alone with him in one of the small meeting rooms. "How are you doing, Horrocks? It's been such a sad time for you."

He murmured, "Yes, it has. I'll have to push my way through it, is all."

"Horrocks…" She nerved herself to ask the terrible question. "Why does your father call you a bastard? I know it's not my business and you don't have to answer."

He stared at her fixedly for a moment and then said in the same low voice as before: "It's been going on for a long time … I made myself believe he loved me. My mother always said he did, even though he didn't love her. I never saw him much, don't remember ever having more than one meal with him, he only sent messages, do this or that, never thanked or praised me when I did it all … I had the weird feeling that the better I did the less he cared for me. But I hid that feeling from myself. I kept telling myself how much he loved me … Before she died my mother told me that he would never admit I was his son, even with all the DNA testing—"

"That was why he called you a bastard? He really believed you were illegitimate?"

"I don't know if you've ever seen my mother—she was a doctor, a pediatrician, quite well known, she worked here in the New World Hospital, maybe even cared for your son."

"Yes—I must have met her."

"You may not remember what she looked like, but I'm the male version, tall, red-haired—"

"Now I do remember—"

"And he felt he had an excuse to disown me because there's nothing of me that's like him. He claimed she faked the DNA test but he settled a lot of money on us. Because…" He swallowed. "I don't know if you've heard of this, but some years ago he went to Barrazan Five with a crew who were hoping to terraform so the Meshar would have a safer place to live, and Xanthrotek would be working on crop-growing and fertilizing, and, and, I don't know why but he fell in love with a Meshar woman, and—"

He was finding it hard to speak the words.

"I heard some rumors."

"Yes, and … he wanted to have a child by her, and because of the work we were doing for the Shar, he demanded that Xanthrotek do whatever it took to make it happen."

"Oh…"

"No, I wouldn't touch that, and he couldn't make anyone else at

Xanthrotek do it either, though he had a bunch of hangers-on who came around and threatened us … it's an immoral idea—alien chimeras!—and so far impossible to do … it would be evil even if it was possible. Then Delius asked me why I seemed to be so down and I felt I had to say something, so I told a lie and said I was afraid I couldn't live up to my father's expectations—but that was true enough, when he always expected me to fail and I didn't."

"Thank yourself for that!"

"Yes, but—" he took a deep breath, "—in a way I became afraid of succeeding and I had to fight that, fight wanting anything from him. About a year ago my mother told me his Meshar woman had died, and I think maybe she was hoping she could get closer to him—she really did love him, you know, in spite of everything—and I didn't say anything to her, but I knew that would never happen."

He fell silent, and she regarded him with a rising sense of dread. In the windowless room the sickly grey walls closed in.

He murmured, "And now the signal of that Meshar woman, Ruah, has gone missing…"

She felt dizzy. "Horrocks … he sent you out to fail all those times! Is it possible that he wanted this project—"

He stared at her, turned white and said angrily, "Yes, isn't it? How could I ever tell that to anybody?"

She took a deep breath. "You don't have to say anything, Horrocks, because there's no proof, and you have nothing to be guilty about. This is just a conjecture, and I'm sorry I brought it up."

Horrocks said grimly, "I'm not feeling guilty. The subject had to come up sooner or later."

❧ ❧

Leaving, Natalya touched his hand and could do no more. She hurried away, grabbed James out of the crèche and hugged him fiercely.

"What's all that love for all of a sudden?" James asked calmly.

"I needed it."

But she got little sleep that night.

* * E L E V E N * *

THE WORLD SHAR:

CAPITAL CITY EQUATORIAL LANDS

AESH DEEP IN

The door smashed open, Aesh felt a sting and cried out, a light pierced his eyes. "What—"

"Just to hold on to you, Aesh-lord!" a rasping voice said in *lingua,* and Aesh remembered how he had been stung to keep him from *shifting* in zero gravity when he was called up to visit the aliens in orbit. Two pairs of hands gripped him. "Where's the other one!"

The corner Sefer had slept in was empty. *Shifted?* Or simply deserted. "Your landlord told us there were two!" the voice said. The innkeeper his father had trusted.

Voice number two said, "It doesn't matter. This is the one we want."

"Let me up," Aesh said. A headache hit him as if an iron crown had been dropped on his head.

Two hands under the armpits hoicked him up. "What do you want?" His voice seemed distant and separate. The headache, or the needle numbed him. Light flashed and made him squint at these unknowns. The anti-*shifting* drug handled by Shar. An interesting thought to consider, if he lived that long.

One to each side they grasped his arms. "What made you think the people would fight for you!" To his dizzy head it seemed that they both spoke at once through snarling teeth.

The street outside the door was very quiet: then lightning split the sky and rain began.

"Let go of my arms," he said, instead of: *What did you pay the landlord?* Though he was beyond frightened, he wanted to stay alive. They loosened their hold, barely. "What people? I never asked anybody to fight for me."

The hands tightened. "The noise in the streets should tell you. The Council will have something to say to you!"

The reddish dawn was rising in the sky, but it did not stop the rain.

"I haven't anything to tell the Council."

"You told those fools in the streets, if they caused trouble they'd get their way. You're coming with us!" The one at his right arm reached outside the doorway and drew in a cage of wooden slabs and bars. Running on steel rollers that rattled over the rough floor, it was a piece of basic alien technology that went with the stinger, and it was the nearest thing to a prison on Shar.

Before Aesh could say another word one of the strangers opened the cage door and the other pushed him in, grabbed an armful of his belongings and tossed them in after, then flung the door shut. The clang reverberated in the iron ring of his headache.

As they pushed the cage outside Aesh could see that his landlord was lying by the doorway. He stirred a little as they passed. Not dead, at least. If he was a betrayer, he had not been well rewarded.

His captors made a show of wheeling the cage down the street, giving it a splashing twirl occasionally and sniggering a bit, but did not abuse him otherwise. They were city officials by their armbands, doing an errand for the Council, and might even have been appointed by Ohr.

Aesh managed to get his feet into the clogs and grasped the bars. He himself had ordered felons into cages, and was not sorry for that. The cage subdued them quickly, even without drugs. He felt subdued enough. But the men running in the streets on their way to work, hunched in the rain, did not recognize him.

There was a great scattering of debris in the streets from the night's rioting: stones, broken staffs, small dead animals. Other workers, city officials, were scurrying about with barrows and brooms sweeping up the refuse and clumps of mud along with it. The air was filled with the bitter reek of wet matter.

His captors began to run; the rain hit him now, under the roofing, the cage rattled and squeaked, the shabby buildings of the area went by quickly, but not so quickly that he did not catch sight of the body of an unwoman lying crouched in the rubbish, flung out of the doorway of a building where the old were sent to die.

He was hit by a lightning-stroke of horror and then guilt, as if he had committed a crime, become a felon, while the rattling cage intensified his headache.

Then he was at the gate. One of the officials pushing the cage yelled, "Hey-yah!" and ran his staff along its bars to make them ring.

Aesh's old friend/enemy, the Chief of Guards, opened the gate as the cage was unlocked, and stared. "You fools, what have you got him in there for? Come out, Aesh-lord, I will bring you your clothes."

Aesh stepped out carefully. The Chief of Guards looked hard at him and muttered, "They gave you that drug." He slammed the cage's door forcefully enough to send it rolling down the lane and make the officials run after it, but they did not dare start an argument with him.

Aesh said, "Who were those men that caged me?"

"Never saw them before. The new Emperor chose them for the City, I expect." He added, "This is my last tenday on duty. The Council shucked me too. Not enough loyalty for them."

"And who is Emperor now?

"Eh, they picked Arvig, because he looks safe, but his son Ayin would like a try at it, if he can't get Givor elected—he's Givor's plaything, you know."

"No, I didn't know that."

"You never gossiped."

"No. Others didn't gossip when I was near."

"I don't want to do this, but I must take you inside the courtyard, or they'll be dragging me into the cage." He paused. "If you want to know about Sefer, he *shifted* here and I pushed him into the doctors' office."

"What happened?"

"When those fools came along he thought the Polar Monarchy was coming to kill him because of some old business and nearly died of fright, or so he said."

"It may be he was right." Aesh said. His captors had asked, *Where's the other one?*

The Chief of Guards closed the gate. It rang harder than the cage. "Here are your staff and your tunic, Aesh-lord. You were the Emperor."

The guards in the courtyard went about their work and did not look at Aesh as he changed clothes.

%%%

The Council members turned themselves on their benches to look at him. He was given a seat at an angle of the savaged table, a little apart from their circle.

Finally, old Arvig bent toward him and said in his gritty voice, "Aesh, seed of Ohr, you are here today because you have been accused of stirring up riot in this city and its territories. What do you have to say for yourself?"

Aesh said, "Let me first say that I was wakened by having my door smashed open, then drugged, roughly handled, and put in a cage, when I would have come willingly if asked. Let the Archivist take note of that." It was quiet here now, and the headache began to ebb.

"Noted."

"Good. A group of people came to me at my father's house and said that they were exhausted from caring for the mothers. They asked me what I was going to do, because I had made promises to restore women and nothing had come of them. I told them I had been unable to keep those promises, that they must come to speak to their Council, yourselves, but take care not to become angry or strike out."

"Will you swear to that?"

Ayin cried out, "Be careful how you swear! Two men were killed and many wounded in the rioting last night! You can be caged in the Public Square and shunned for that!"

"For what? Telling them not to be angry?"

"You must have told them very softly if they didn't listen!"

"If I had been angry with them they would likely have struck out at me. But I'm not afraid to swear to the truth of what I say, and I am speaking truth."

The Councillors murmured among themselves, these men Aesh had known for many years.

Ayin suddenly looked up at him and said, "There will be burials and cleansing rites, some of the wounded will die, and there will be half a year's healing. You may even be killed for this, you know."

Aesh knew, yes, if Ayin had his way. If he were Emperor.

Ayin added, "There are places in our world where sacrifices are still made to the Angry-God—"

In a low and penetrating voice, Arvig broke through: "Not in our land!"

In a moment of uncomfortable silence a messenger entered the Council chamber. Arvig crooked his forefinger in admission and the messenger hissed words in his ear.

Arvig stiffened, and sat rigid for several moments. Then sent the messenger off and said, "This meeting will be put off now, until I call it again. The guard nearest me will take Aesh, son of Ohr, to the waiting-hall for food and shelter in the meantime."

DELIUS IN THE ORBIT OF SHAR:

Delius, clothed in shadow-grey cylon, looked down at the dark world crackling with lightning. No moons circled this planet: it seemed as if Angry-God had declared it unworthy, muffled it in clouds, fouled its air. The orbiting storehouses and offices, shaped like titanic eggs, were its only substitute for moons, and they reflected little light.

Despite Semdah's insistence that he must become an authority fig-ure, Delius could not bring himself to parade as one, decked out in gold braid again. But everything he had thought last time he was here, he thought again. *You do too damned much deep thinking, Delius,* says Genever. The many things the Shar had been promised, the few that GalFed had managed to do.

The *Zarandu* had delivered him and his crew, with Kohav, to the main station of the orbit. He had a fairly good view of several other of the ovoid units, and there were many. Galactic Federation kept a basic station with a minor envoy and clerical staff here, and he checked in briefly with a nod to a couple of grizzled veterans; most other offices were small head-quarters for big corporations, except for the few great loading stations: some of the Federation employees were women, and for a short while they seemed almost alien to Delius, cleaner and fresher than the crews he had to hang about with.

He had spent several hours waiting for shuttle transport for his diplomatic visit to Xanthrotek's headquarters, in the company of Varvani, Bimandans, and other Earthers with various kinds of breathing tanks or filters, on their way to diverse errands. Dos Ramos had come from somewhere in this orbit; someone in it had given the order to kill him. He wondered briefly about the agent Semdah had hidden away, but was content not to know where.

He had only a few words to say to anyone here. Mick and Jacko were dozing in their seats, oblivious to the noise of the gravitors. Their hum was everywhere, and Delius noticed that some employees wore earplugs. The sight of those reminded him of his nose filters, which were as irritating as usual, to say nothing of the oxycap behind his ear.

When his shuttle call finally came, there was only one seating for him, and he did not bother disturbing his sleepers. He crawled down between the grey plasmix walls of the corridor and into the emergency suit to breathe the even staler oxygen than the cabin's. He had switched off the oxycap to save it for Shar's atmosphere.

There was a dull and much noisier hour in the shuttle. Xanthrotek was stationed in the greatest of the eggs, and shared it with several warehouses, so that there were more corridors lit by dim lights. A fellow passenger directed him to the suite of offices, enmeshed in a complex of grubby corridors.

He exchanged civilities with a sub-director of the company, praised its efforts, expressed regrets, promised fair treatment, and hoped for the future. Much the same work as he had been doing on many of those far-off worlds. No whisper about how a Meshar woman disappeared into the estate of the company's retiring CEO, nor any way to mention Dos Ramos. Only the luxury of removing his nose-filters and breathing musty but real air.

There was nothing impressive about the place. Several of its work-cells were empty. He wondered if the news of the explosion had spread, and how far.

He left Xanthrotek in time to meet the next shuttle, and followed the way back as he remembered it.

Halfway there, he stopped, hit by a peculiar smell, sweet, almost spicy...

His mind said *Shar.* At the same time, he realized that he had forgotten to replace the nose plugs and reached for the case where he kept them. Then his mind said *Shar here?*

A Shar jumped at him out of a doorway, one arm reaching for his neck and the other holding a knife. In the familiar dialect, he snarled, "One alien too many!"

Before the claws could grasp or the knife stab, Delius slammed down on the arms with the edges of both hands, and kicked one of the knees with his heavy boot.

The Shar fell back and folded up in pain for a moment, twitching and whimpering, then *shifted.*

Delius was bewildered. Shar might be brought up to be treated for diseases, but not this one, in the doorway of a mining office, and with a weapon in his hand. He stared at the knife on the floor, but did not touch it.

And Delius ... I pray you have no enemies, Semdah had said. He began to shiver, and pushed away at fear.

But he hurried away, stuffing the filters into his nostrils as he went.

He thought of Mick and Jacko. But what could they have done? Mick had a prosthetic hand with three weapons built into it, but no permission to use them. And the Shar was a scrawny underling without weapons.

Back in the shuttle he spent the hour wondering why there had been a Shar in this place. A memory flickered in his mind's eye: *Not all of us want these damned aliens!* When he had used that "iron bar of an arm" to defend Genever. The voice was the same, but so were a lot of Shar voices to his inexperienced hearing. And this one Shar had changed his allegiance quickly, and was prepared to serve aliens, evidently, and attack them if he had been ordered ... Dos Ramos's murderer? Dos Ramos had been a Galactic Federation agent. Perhaps the Shar was someone else's.

Or perhaps someone believed he, Delius, was replacing Dos Ramos.

Delius forced his mind away from those thoughts.

Back in the station there was nothing more he could do now than take a doze in a hammock for a round or two while the Councillors of the Equatorial Lands were informed of their visitors. When he woke he found Mick and Jacko yawning and muttering, the biologist Cobb beside them, staring down toward the world. Kohav had moved away, intent on his own thoughts.

A worker on a ten-minute break came over.

"Ugly looking place. Can't think how you'd really want to go down there." The language here was English. These workers were uneasy with aliens.

Delius said quietly, "Lots of people have gone down from here…" And spoke the name. "Dos Ramos didn't mind."

And some are ready to come up here too.

"Yeh. Good fellow." Clearing of throat. "We had your friend Aesh up here one time."

"Was he impressed?"

"Not with us. Hard-nosed little bastard."

And what about that other one?

When he was gone, Delius said to Cobb, "I know Mick and Jacko here are my heavy handlers. What's your assignment, Cobb?" Cobb was still a stranger.

"I do the same work as Horrocks," Cobb said. "He was intended to be here instead of me, but Semdah wanted him. Assignment?" He twisted his face into thoughtful contortions. "You could say I'm looking for a 'lusus naturae.'"

"Freak of nature? Eh, I haven't heard Latin since I escaped from the Academy. Can you tell me what it is?"

"I can tell you I'll know it when I see it."

"Too bad you weren't with us in Meshar country on Barrazan Five."

"I was on Oerstmann Six finishing up on Horrocks's work in a situation much like it. You know how Semdah moves us around like chess pieces."

"Exactly."

"Dunno if I'll run into you before we leave. I'll be doing my work in small populations."

"Glad I met you, then."

Cobb dropped into his linking capsule and Delius was left to wonder what in the world he was looking for.

Then the thought of Aesh flickered over him, a dark shadow. *I know what I'm looking for. So far I've found more than I wanted.*

Kohav whispered, "I want to see my son."

SHAR:

CAPITAL CITY

A satellite-controlled landcar was waiting at the port to take Delius and company into the city; it was a long ride, skittering gravel behind it to the city's edge, then hissing over the cobbles. There was an astonishing amount of rubbish in the streets: stones, broken staffs, small dead animals. A glimpse—Delius thought he must be mistaken—of a dead unwoman half-buried in trash. Scores of Shar were working their ways through it with brushes and wheelbarrows in a slow and dispirited way.

Kohav said, with a tremor in his voice, "Something terrible has happened here."

It was midday and the red sun, like a hot coal, burned its way through the thick atmosphere of the ochre sky. On many worlds that Delius had visited, colonists were fighting their way through unbridled growth. Around the shores of the islands the foliage grew deeper and richer; in this area of Shar there was little but a fierce vegetation of twisting ivies with woody bent-knuckled stems covering the uninhabited tracts, and here in the city most of them forced their way out between the cobbles and the bases of the clay-bricked buildings. A few broom-thin trees raised branches above buildings that were never higher than three storeys.

On his first visit he had seen nothing of these surroundings; his contingent had been hurriedly stuffed into the quarters attached to the Council complex

It was spring here now, and most of the ivy knuckles bore small yellow globes that were popping with powdery seed. Some had been smashed by the force of whatever conflict had been going on before Delius came, and their fragments glimmered among the cobbles.

His one visit to Earth years ago had been for the purpose of easing new settlers and worn retirees exercising their Right of Return, into shabby and forgotten cities. This place brought back those memories. The civilization, Shar, was an ancient one, but its old cities were small towns, and the dark fur and tails of its inhabitants gave it an almost prehistoric look. Among them Delius was feeling white as bleached bone.

He quickly pulled himself out of this frame of mind; it was worthy of an amateur, and Delius was none of that. But he could not help thinking of those faded cities on his ancestral world, and feeling the force of his own over-rich surroundings on Fthel IV in the glistening body of the landcar.

He thought of stopping the machine and walking the rest of the way, but that kind of act belonged to his past, and preparing to face the Emperor and his Council, he had no time for proletarian gestures. Particularly on rough cobbled streets.

Delius's Observer days were over, he knew that now, and he had unwillingly been recreated as a diplomat. One with an annoying oxycap and itching nose filters.

꧁꧂

The Council was waiting for him as it had done in the hot noon of his first visit.

In the still air among the shafts of red sunlight, the present Emperor of the Lands, Arvig, sat with his thirty-nine Councillors at the council table. The great burled hexagon had a roughly mended slash in its center. Behind the men a half-circle of guards stood leaning on their staffs.

In the focus of all those pairs of onyx eyes swimming in red membranes, grey-eyed Delius would have preferred not to be the sole representative of Galactic Federation on the world Shar. That was not quite the case: Mick and Jacko were standing behind him at the doorways, and Kohav as well, but they were small match for the forty and more figures of authority.

Delius bowed with clasped hands, as he had done before Aesh long ago.

A guard brought a bench and set it at one of the angles of the table.

"Sit," Arvig said. "Peter Delius, representative of Galactic Federation, why are you here?"

"I made an oath to the Emperor and this world." He spoke in the local vernacular.

"That was another Emperor." Arvig's face was not angry or threatening, and Delius sensed some discomfort in it.

"It doesn't cancel my oath," he said.

Not quite humoring him, Arvig said, "And what great oath did you swear, tell me?"

"That I would do my best to see that Galactic Federation kept its promises. To restore women, make the companies in the sky treat you fairly, help you to grow food, weave cloth, treat diseases. Strengthen you to help you build up your world."

"There are no records of this oath having been sworn."

"The Emperor made me swear not to tell. Because many promises have been made and solemn oaths sworn by many parties in the multi-octads of your history—but never kept. And now I have to confess that the Federation as well has been unable to keep my oath."

"Why are you telling this secret now, Envoy?"

"Because there was no harm in his asking or in my promising. His action was innocent, he wanted good treatment for his country and his world, he asked nothing for himself. But he did not want to seem a beggar in the eyes of others."

"And Galactic Federation would rather deal with that Emperor?"

"The Federation respects the choices of the worlds that have joined with it. We also want to know that he has been fairly treated by a people who have created a civilization for themselves in the face of so much labor and sorrow."

Arvig's black-and-red eyes flickered. "So many words to ask so little. We have not harmed Aesh, who was Emperor."

"Then why is he not free to speak with me? What wrong has he done?"

"His words caused violence."

"Has he told you this?"

"He denies it."

"Why do you not believe him?"

"Haven't you looked around yourself coming through the city? Were there not signs of violence, destruction, death?"

"I saw them clearly enough. Caused by one man who left the office of his own free will? Who accuses him?"

"Those who have been bloodied."

"Why were they fighting?"

"Some want women restored, and others do not."

"I understand," Delius said. "And where are the ones who struck the first blows last night if I may ask, Arvig-lord?"

There was a moment of blank silence. "They have not yet been found."

"But Aesh-lord has been accused."

"So has it been reported to me. I must add, Peter Delius, that it is our right to act according to our own laws and practices and not yours."

"I beg your pardon. Then let me ask: what do you intend to do for the people in this part of the world, your people?"

"What do you expect me to tell you?"

"What do you want Galactic Federation to do? Work to restore your women? Leave you to live out your lives without them? Which? I know that you have the power to rule in any way that you consider right, and I have not come to interfere, but to find how Galactic Federation can help."

"And why is it so important! And at this time? I'm not sure that you truly admit that I have the power, if you have come to tell me what I ought to do!"

A fist slammed the table and a louder voice cried, "Why have you come, then, alien!"

Delius had studied them all in his orbispex, and knew that this was Givor. He bent forward and said quietly, "Please excuse me for reminding you, but your people are fighting each other in the streets over this question, and that, you have told me, is why you have blamed and seized Aeshlord. But he is not a threat to you. What is truly dangerous is that the number of people in this world is shrinking. Of every octad one less will be born in every generation. We have found that your people are in more danger than we knew."

A much louder voice said, "And in the future every one will be as sterile as I, my three daughters and my son Aesh. That will be the end of our people."

The Council looked up from the seated Delius, and he turned to see the father of Aesh, accompanied by a guard with a crossbow slung from his shoulder. Several of the Council guards had begun to aim their spears at him, then, recognizing who he was, lowered them.

Arvig clicked his tongue because the Chief of Guards should have announced Ohr's coming and asked permission to let him in, but he said nothing.

Givor said harshly, "You come to plead for your son, I suppose?"

Ohr said, more mildly, "As you would for yours, old friend. The more time we waste in anger the more quickly our people will shrink and die." He turned to address himself to the Emperor. "Arvig-lord, tell us as well as this envoy what you will do to restore our people."

Arvig took a deep breath. "First I will do everything possible to bring peace. There is nothing to be done without it. But you must keep the peace until we decide what course to take with your son Aesh. And the Council won't be able to do that in your presence."

"I will leave. But first let me see my son."

Arvig looked at him reflectively; Ohr had been his closest friend. "You may see your son."

Ayin said, "Arvig-lord, do you know what you are doing?"

"Yes, Ayin-seed. We are examining Aesh, not yet convicting him. Excuse me, Peter Delius, while I do my best to settle this local matter. Would you take a seat further back until we finish?"

Delius at once moved back to sit with his company. Beside him, Kohav gripped his arm and cried out, "I want my son!"

Arvig leaned forward, working to focus his white-streaked eyes. "Kohav, is it? It's good to find you safe. One of the guards will go home with you and you will have your son." He crooked his finger at the nearest guard: "You will go with Kohav to the Mother-Hall where his son is kept."

"No!" Kohav said, with a tinge of panic. "I want Aesh-lord to come with me! The child will not know me without him."

Arvig stared at him, dumfounded. It seemed as if Kohav had heard nothing of what had been said before. Or what had happened to his Emperor.

"Aesh cannot go with you right now." Arvig could not quite bring himself to say that Aesh, Kohav's Emperor, was an accused felon. There were stirrings behind him and he turned his head quickly and said, "Be still!" and turning back, "Kohav, you must go home until the matter is set right, and you will have your son. I swear." He waited until one of the guards escorted Kohav out across the courtyard. Then Arvig looked at

Delius with perplexity as he gestured at him to come forward.

"It appears you have come to shame us, in pointing out all that you believe we have done wrong."

Delius drew upon endless patience. "No, no, Arvig-lord! I meant only that we want to help. The Equatorial Lands is the greatest nation here, and most likely the others will follow your example. And though there are many federations in the Galaxy, no other has offered to restore your people. We want to honor Aesh-lord for being the first to agree that the help we offered was necessary and right. Because that work was destroyed by an evil person does not make Aesh-lord unworthy."

"I understand you, Peter Delius, and we will discuss this fully, but it is late now and the darkness is rising. We need rest and food. But first, guard! Yes, you! Bring out Aesh son of Ohr so that his father and Galactic Federation can see that he has not been harmed."

The guard returned with Aesh, obviously taking care not to touch him. The thirty-nine Councillors sat like stone. But Aesh stood where the guard left him.

Ohr took two steps forward, and no more. Arvig demanded, "Have you been harmed, Aesh seed of Ohr?"

"I've been roughly handled, but not beaten," Aesh said calmly.

Ohr said, with increasing anger, "Aesh-seed, swear to me that you did nothing to bring this treatment on yourself!"

Aesh said with angry defiance, "I swear on my life! Don't you know your only son after all these years?" And added sadly, "All of this trouble. I did nothing wrong, and see what came of that."

Ohr, drained, said, "I know my only son, and I would never have deserted you, whatever happened."

Bosor moved to Ohr's side, and murmured in his ear.

Arvig said sharply, "Speak up! We're not dealing in secrets here."

Bosor said in a timid voice far removed from his height and strength, "My name is Bosor, and I guard Aesh-lord's father Ohr. I was standing behind Aesh-lord when he spoke to those angry ones, and can tell you every word he said."

"You can? Tell us, then."

"Yes I will. His father, my master, told me to watch out for Aesh-lord because those men were screaming that he had not done enough for them and my master was afraid they would attack Aesh-lord, and—"

A group of Councillors cried out, "We've heard all that already, Arvig-lord!"

"This man Bosor was not here when you heard it," Arvig said. "Speak up, Bosor."

Bosor took a deep breath and said: "Aesh-lord did not know I was listening. With an arrow in my bow. That leader said how hard their lives were when they had to get children from those—those dead things and that fewer sons were being born of them, and Aesh-lord said, 'I can't create women for you,' and told them they should gather a few among them who would speak to you people and they were to be very careful not to get angry. And I will recognize that leader if I see him again." He stopped for lack of breath.

"Good. We will continue this meeting tomorrow. The evening meal will be served in the courtyard."

Ohr and Bosor watched Aesh as he was returned to his imprisonment. "I hope I told them the right thing," Bosor said.

"You did."

"They will think I was doing it to please you."

"You told them truly what you saw and heard, and they can think what they please."

The Councillors grumbled together for some time, but their discussion was peaceable enough as they rose from their table and moved on to their dinners.

❧❧

Delius, socketed into his own stone cell and relieved to remove the filters once more, savored the coolness of the air. "I don't think old Arvig will be too hard on Aesh. I hope not. He seems a lot smarter and stronger than he looked at first."

"He wasn't afraid to jump on those Councillors," Jacko said. "He had to do that when there was somebody like Ohr in front of him."

"The rest of the Council table may not care much for what he did," Delius said. "From what I gather, Arvig is supposed to be a safe one, a harmless idiot. The file on the orbispex claims he was voted in because the others wanted to avoid Givor. I wish Arvig had that big Bosor guarding him."

"Bosor matches Ohr, and Ohr is a somebody!" Mick said. "He seems to grow bigger when he talks. Aesh has to work hard having him for a father."

"Aesh and his siblings are sterile," Delius murmured. "I hadn't known that until I found it on the orbispex … that must make him feel smaller than he looks."

His eyes were sore from the prickling air, and when he closed them the frieze on the tower wall spread itself before the darkness. *A way of becoming whole. The way.*

"Was this food left here from the last time we came?" Mick stared into his bowl and pushed it into the recycle chute. He stood up and tried to stretch, pushing at the ceiling as if he could lift it. "There's no room to move here." He dug in his backpack for the filters. "I'm going out."

Jacko said. "You better watch it. You can't tell them you're doing it for the fresh air."

"Right!" Delius said, "And if you fire off any of those things you've got built in, you're out of here and out of work."

Mick snarled, "Just in the hallway to stretch my legs! I'm not gonna get in the way of all the Shar out there."

But as soon as he pushed the leather curtain aside, all three of them heard the shouting. Delius stuffed the damned filters into his nostrils again and followed the other two out of the quarters, now running across the courtyard.

There were uncleared trestles here of half-eaten food, dinner for guards and Councillors both, but no one ate of it now.

The Councillors were milling about trying to stay out of the way of the crew of Emperor's guards and servants surging furiously around the tower. The Chief of Guards was rushing up the steps crying out, "Come down, Arvig-lord, come down!" Another stood in the archway, brandishing a spear at someone outside, whom Delius could not see in the evening mist.

Then, against the deep red sky, he caught sight of a figure moving on the ledge of the roof connecting with the tower. It was a Shar, no one he could recognize in that dimness, who stopped for a moment and then

*

appeared again beside the tower window.

Delius stared. "Is Arvig there?"

Someone answered, "He went to clean himself for dinner."

Here on the roof was a come-and-go *shifter* who could move as he chose. But he could carry no weapons while he *shifted,* and wear no clothing. *Shift* and *shift*—his body flickered there-and-gone, like lightning. Three guards with crossbows shot at him and missed.

From the roof's ledge where he was standing, the Shar picked up a spear and took aim through Arvig's window—

A flicker in Delius's mind: *Weapon planted there. Insider.*

Without asking permission, Mick raised his prosthetic hand, flicked off the tip of his forefinger, a needle extended from it, he pointed, it whirred and pierced—

The Shar turned his head, stopped and stared down at the needle in his chest, eyes wide and mouth open. Dropped the spear, gaping in terror: flickered, disappeared

*

then burst head and arms out of the stone wall, shrieked once and died in a slather of blood and an explosion of stone chips.

In the midst of the great outcry of the horrified guards and servitors swarming about, ducking the burst of splinters, Mick bent over, retching and shuddering. "Not me, I didn't mean to kill him! The needle was for stopping the *shift*, I was just trying to hold him down." He was clumsily recapping his finger, unable to stop shaking.

Delius gaped at him. "Who in God's name gave you that drug?"

"It came in my orbispex package," Mick whispered, and repeated, "I didn't mean to kill him."

Delius muttered, "He really meant to kill Arvig."

Packed with the orbispex? A likely story. He found himself gritting his teeth. *But it was the needle that saved Arvig. Now who sent that little bastard Shar to kill him? And why?*

He looked up. The lights in the tower flickered, and in a few moments Arvig came down the steps, falteringly. His Councillors turned him away from that wall, and whether they loved him or not, gathered round to comfort him. He stared at Mick.

"You saved my life, and I'm happy to be alive, but that was a terrible way for a man to die…" He called out, "Everyone! I have twisted my leg trying to escape, but I am not wounded." Arvig pulled away from their grasping arms and limped across the courtyard, grimacing, obviously forcing himself to examine the remains of the *shifter.*

Arvig said, "Who knows this one? Can anyone tell me?"

The Bengtvadi doctor who had his office in the far corner came over with a young Shar to examine the face. "I don't know," he said, "but this young man might."

The Shar wanted to pull away, but the Bengtvad grasped his arm. Arvig examined him and said, "Who are you, young one?"

The young one looked him in the eye and said, "I am Sefer and I guard Aesh-lord."

Arvig pulled up the dead Shar's head by one ear and said, "Look at this face! Do you know this man?"

After a careful moment, Sefer suppressed a shiver and said, "I can't swear to it, but he looks to me like the one that killed the Earther Dos Ramos. This red scar over my eye is what he did to me when I tried to stop him."

Delius thought of the Shar in orbit leaping out with his knife.

The Bengtvadi murmured, "Ah yes, he was the one who attacked you in orbit." For once Delius forgave an intrusion into his mind.

"But why was there a Shar in orbit?"

"An agreement with the Commercials: symbolic watchman, a Shar privilege."

Delius muttered, "They damned well didn't watch the one they chose."

Arvig was speaking more calmly. "We have a deal of thinking to do. We will meet again tomorrow as planned … but first let us finish our dinner." He clicked his fangs and turned his back on the wall.

Delius and company left them to it and returned to their lodgings in a hurry.

"Cold-blooded, I call that one! I'm glad I'm not eating out there." Mick shook himself once more and regained his usual impudence: "Are you going to discharge me, mister Delius?"

"Some other time."

THE SERPENT'S TOOTH

Another session in the Council Hall: Delius did not believe that the night had gone well for anyone. It seemed to him that Arvig's fur had become more deeply streaked with white, but he also felt that his own perception was influenced by the obvious strain in Arvig's face and manner. Outside in the courtyard a noisy group of alien workmen, Earthers and others, had been called in to clear away the bloody rubbish of flesh and stones.

Arvig, occasionally sticking a finger in one ear to dull the sounds, said, "Before we take up our discussion regarding Aesh seed of Ohr, I want to ask," he bent down to the spear lying hidden under the table and raised it, "who owns this?"

No answer.

"Do I need to ask who owns this spear?"

He flung it away and it landed with a clatter on the stone floor.

Ayin picked it up from where it had fallen beside his foot. "I don't own a spear, Arvig-lord. Spears are carried by our guards."

Arvig faced him. "Someone needed to come into the tower's chamber with this spear to reach out of the window and place it on the roof ledge of the Council House. No self-*shifter* could carry one. No guard comes in without permission. No one recognized the *shifter* except the doctor who esped him and that young guard whom I didn't know and who was under the doctor's watch all the time. Who else but my son could come into that room without being stopped?"

Delius was thinking of the Bengtvadi doctor, the low-grade telepath who was just powerful enough to know ... and was not afraid to tell. He had better watch out, that Bengtvad.

Ayin said in a low voice, "I never meant to kill you. Only to drive you out."

The Councillors pushed back their benches and stared at him

"Frighten me," Arvig said. "is that it? My own son, you are such a great fool!" He clutched his chest tightly enough to pull the guardhairs out. "Aiyah, the Angry-God has got me now! Guards! You and you there! *Unshift* my son and remove him to some safe place that I don't know of."

But Ayin broke away from their reach and stumbled around the table to grab Givor by the shoulders. "For you!" he howled. "I did it for you!"

Givor pulled free in horror. "You are a fool! How could you think I would want that! Did you truly believe that wounding your father would make me Emperor after all the years I have sat here without being chosen? Have I ever asked to be chosen?"

Ayin said no more and let the guards take him.

Arvig stared at Delius and said in a crumbling voice, "Galactic Federation has saved me from my own son!" He turned to Ohr, who had been watching Arvig's shame with nearly as much agony as if it had been his own. "Now we will deal with your son."

Ohr stood and stepped forward to touch Arvig's forehead with his thumb. "Let us stop. You cannot go on in such pain."

"I cannot stop, or my pain will swallow me."

"Believe me, I am not afraid for my son, because I know your judgement will be fair."

"It will," Arvig said grimly, and called, "Bring me the Chief of Guards!"

The Chief of Guards came in looking as if he expected to have his thumbs twisted. He stood leaning on his staff and waiting.

Arvig said, "Watchman, on the day that Aesh son of Ohr was carried here in a cage, did you give the order for that seizure?"

"I did not. The ones that came wore armbands that claimed them to be City officials. I didn't recognize them and I assumed that the Civic Officer sent them."

Arvig said sharply, "Citizen Ohr can tell you that Civic officials have nothing to do with collecting suspects our Council is looking for."

"Should I have insisted that Aesh son of Ohr, who was Emperor, be delivered to a cell in Civic Hall?"

"I'm not blaming you, you acted correctly. I only wish you could have recognized those so-called officials."

Delius was thinking: *I'd swear that son of his sent them … no use tormenting Arvig with that.*

"They may be real ones," the Chief of Guards said. "If they are, their cage must belong to the City, and I'll ask the Civic Officer about who was allowed to use it. I sent them away in a hurry, and if I find them I'll tie their tails in knots for them."

"Good. You are no longer removed from duty, and will go on with your work as Chief of Guards."

The Chief of Guards bowed without comment and left. He was no lickspit. But many of the Councillors were muttering.

Delius caught the words as Ohr hissed in Arvig's ear, "You need better personal guards."

"Yes. Find me a Bosor." Arvig took a deep breath and gestured. "Now, you there, bring out Aesh son of Ohr."

Aesh was brought out, once more, carefully. He seemed worn and uncaring, his fur ruffled and his shoulders slack. He saw Ohr looking hard at him, and made some effort to straighten himself and appear defiant.

Arvig said, "One more time, Aesh, son of my oldest friend, tell us what happened after you left your father's house."

Aesh said wearily, "A group of angry people stopped me and my guard, I told them to sort out a small group and speak to the Council— *quietly*. They let us go by. They were upset because their lives were so hard, but they were not violent.

"I and my guard went to a lodging my father had said was a good one. At midnight some men I didn't know broke down the door and stunned me with anti*shift* but my guard was caught by surprise and *shifted* before they could take him. I could see that there had been rioting in the streets. Those men threw me into a cage and were spinning and knocking the cage about until I reached here, then the Chief of guards stopped that and took me in. He thought those men had been hired by you."

"Is there anything else you wish to say?"

"No, except again, that I have done nothing wrong."

Arvig raised his voice as loud as his old lungs would let him. "All you out there within hearing, tell us what great harm Aesh son of Ohr has done you—or disperse!"

But though there was a great muttering, some cries of "Free him!" and some of "Torch him" and other imprecations, Delius felt that most of the people, from the weary Councillors and guards, to the hangers-on at the fences, were simply at this point enjoying the drama that gave their lives a rare bit of flavor.

Arvig stood, raised his arms and kept them up. "There are no witnesses to show that the accused broke any law. For no reason he was treated like a wild beast. If there was a crime, that was it. Aesh son of Ohr is free." He sat. "Now it may be that we can go on discussing the state of the world. But we will not begin that until tomorrow."

There was a flurry of angry muttering among the guards, and Arvig turned and cried out wearily, "Who opened the gate, and what is this, now! What more trouble can we have?"

A voice called, "We ask permission to speak to the Emperor!"

Three men stood in the courtyard, flanked by the Chief of Guards and another. One of the three with a bronze-tipped staff, the other two with crossbows, and over the shoulder of each, the skin of a northern turbu, white with black zigzags, like negatives of lightning.

Arvig said, "I recognize the accents, Polar Monarchy, and I must have met you—yes, you, Zagbin-lord, on your visit here five years ago." Panting, he needed deep breaths for the effort of pronouncing gracious words to cover his pain.

"Yes, Arvig-lord. We made a very satisfactory trade agreement on that occasion with your management under the former emperor." He turned toward Aesh with a bow.

Arvig made the courtesy-obeisance. "I still regret that our climate is too extremely hot for us to make use of those beautiful turbu skins you produce in the North."

"So do we, but that is not why we came."

"I am listening."

"Our Emperor Khorastax has died—"

"We are distressed to hear that. A great loss…"

"Eh. Yes."

"I presume you have a replacement."

"Yes, our newly elected Emperor Sandek Three sends his greetings, and wants to assure you that all our agreements will be maintained."

"Give him our blessings. I hope we will meet soon."

"I agree. And we also encourage the former Polar citizens now living in this land, to return and enjoy a visit in our renewed nation." For Aesh a slanted message that Sefer was not being hunted. Whoever might be hoping to collect a reward for his capture would be out of luck.

"I will be sure to let them know," Arvig said.

The two sides made obeisance again and the Polar delegation left.

When they were out of earshot, Arvig muttered, "I'm sure the old villain must have poisoned himself between the grind-brew and the dirtweed."

For once his Council agreed with him.

He added, almost as an afterthought, "Aesh, when you visit Kohav I will have the child Shemesh sent to you. And Aesh-seed, along with Ohr-father, you are welcome to take your evening meal with us."

Aesh could not bring himself to speak, and Ohr said, "It is good of you, Arvig-lord, but we need to be home." Ohr took Aesh by the shoulder and drew him out into the miserably hot and foul—but free—air of noon. He said, "Don't be too angry at Arvig," and told him the long story of the night of horror and the betrayal by Ayin.

"I heard some of that in my cell," Aesh said. "I know he's a good man and I'm sad for him." He turned to Bosor. "You did much to free me."

"Not without your father, Aesh-lord."

The Chief of Guards hailed the three of them. "You're freed, Aesh-lord? Stay that way."

"You're rehired? You do the same."

"I wish I'd smashed that cage."

"You did what you could. And you sheltered Sefer as well. Now I can tell him he is free."

KOHAV AND SHEMESH

Kohav lived in a small one-roomed house three streets away from the lodging where Aesh had been seized. His time on Fthel IV in the hospital station among all the doctors, officials and other rude questioners had seemed to him a kind of Angry-God's torment; his return, without Aesh-lord to greet him, very little of a welcome. In payment for his services, Galactic Federation kept his belly full, but so far, like Aesh, he had no work to keep him busy.

And everything had changed. On one side he had neighbors who played on the nose-flute at midnight, and on the other a pair who baked their dirtweed in the coalpot out back, and the stink did not improve his own cooking. Only the few thin trees that gave shade remained the same.

Watching Aesh coming down his street along with Ohr and Sefer, he began to feel the touch of hope. They came up quickly and clasped his hands. "The child will come soon," Ohr said.

And in a few moments they could catch sight of the Emperor's guard leading the child in and out of the dappled shade, and Kohav waited without a breath.

As Ohr made ready to offer money, the guard raised his hands to free the boy and backed away. "Emperor's gift," he murmured, turned and left quickly.

"Eh, glad to be shut of us," Ohr said.

Kohav knelt and opened his arms. "Shemesh," he breathed.

The boy shrank back, only barely remembering even Aesh. He had grown taller since Aesh had last seen him.

The boy peered at Aesh, and then at Kohav.

He cried out, "You are Aesh-lord, my friend?"

"Yes, but no lord now, Shemesh son of Kohav!"

"Who's this, Aesh?" Pointing at Kohav. "Who's this?"

"This is your father, Shemesh! You know his name is Kohav, I've told you about him many times."

"This my father? Then what are you, Aesh?"

Kohav pulled back and said harshly, "He is not your father!" And turned snarling to Aesh. "You! You have stolen my son!"

"Kohav, no!" Ohr said reproachfully.

Aesh said in horror, "No! I would never do such a thing!"

"You sent me away so you could steal him!"

"Steal! Ayeh, Kohav, what a terrible word you strike me with! I spoke with him, played with him. You were closest to me, and I loved him as part of you! I haven't been allowed near him since I left the Tower."

Ohr picked up the child, who was whimpering now, and said sharply, "Your Emperor Aesh Seven has been disgraced, imprisoned and mistreated. When you were gone there was no one here but Aesh to love your son! He gave you to Galactic Federation for the honor of taking part in the rebuilding of our people. Their work failed and the Earther Delius brought you back to keep the boy safe. No one has stolen him. He is yours."

Kohav looked downward and bit the knuckle of his forefinger, as near an apology as a Shar will allow himself.

Ohr passed the child to Aesh, who said, "I love him as if he was mine but I have no right to him. I will never see him again if you want that. Here."

Kohav took his son gingerly, as if the weight of responsibility had only just occurred to him. "No, I see that you did your best to keep him safe. I will share him with you while he grows to understand that he is my son."

✶ ✶ T W E L V E ✶ ✶

ᴱᵀᴴᴱᴸ ᴵⱽ:

HORROCKS AND NATALYA

The day after her only too intimate discussion with Horrocks, and the restless sleep that followed, Natalya took up her usual task, along with Mukherjee, of checking on the health of the Shar and Meshar, and after that, pushed herself to the latest of the endless series of meetings that tried to cobble together plans for new attempts at solving Shar's problem.

In a sense she was standing in for Delius. She had little to do with his superiors, and was content with that, but with Delius gone and Horrocks giving her nightmares…

There was no sign of Horrocks, only his empty chair.

Mbai said, "Where's Horrocks?" No one answered. "Doesn't anyone know where he is? Doctor Beylin, you must have seen him recently?"

"I did," Natalya said, "yesterday afternoon. Then I had to go pick up my son at the crèche."

"We can't get very far without him," Mbai said sharply. "I'll have a thing or two to say to him. We'll wait a few minutes."

Natalya used her wrist comm to call his apartment, as well as his comm, but by some intuition she did not expect an answer, and there was none.

Finally Mbai said, "We may as well call off this meeting. I'm going to make some calls too. But Doctor Beylin, would you come to my office, please? We need to discuss some matters."

Natalya slowly and unwillingly obeyed. With unhurried steps she passed the cubicle where she had seen Kohav's friend and the young woman Levona speaking together. They were there again, as they had been so often, and she paused for a moment to watch them opening their souls to each other. Seeing something more than that ... she paused to make a different call.

᠅

Mbai hated to come out of her office cubicle, where she held absolute sway. But it was not a substitute for home; she kept nothing decorative there, not even pictures of her children. She was hunched at her comm screen: faces flickered on it, moving their lips silently, but she shut off quickly, and removed her earphone.

"Sit down, if you will. I'm not a direct superior of yours, Natalya, but with Delius gone, I hope you can help me with this puzzle. Horrocks has been behaving in a very erratic manner lately, and you are the person here that he speaks to the most."

Natalya said carefully, "Yes, he does like to ... confide in me."

"Believe me, I truly don't want to know everything about his most private life, but it seems to be brought to my attention so often! I sense a lot of his troubles have to do with his relationships with his parents. Particularly his father. I'm no eavesdropper, but I have heard a lot of mutterings from others. He must spill everything to anyone who'll listen, how his father hates him, and the Meshar woman from Barrazan Five and all of it. But he's an adult and he'll have to live with it."

"He knows that."

"I would have sent him out with Delius, but Semdah wanted him here where we could keep an eye on him." Mbai took a deep breath. "So much for that idea. I have people searching for him, but no one has seen him today at all, not even where he eats breakfast. Where would he be, now, and what is he doing?"

Natalya found herself unable to breathe. She pulled air into her lungs with a long-drawn rasp.

Mbai, alarmed suddenly, said, "Are you all right, Natalya?"

Natalya forced the words: "Horrocks believes his father may have destroyed the experiment."

Mbai stared at her. "That's a terrifying thought, Natalya! Are you sure you heard right?"

"After what he told me, I said, 'Is it possible that your father meant to…'"

Mbai bent her massive body forward like a thunder-cloud about to spit lightning. "You tell me every damned word both of you spoke!"

Natalya told her all that she could remember, and that was only too clear. "And I told him he didn't have to do anything, because there was no proof, and it was just a conjecture."

"You're right, there is no evidence." Mbai clenched her teeth with a click. "But it fits," she said. "We suspected the old man got hold of our Meshar woman. Her signal winked out near the Vanbrennan estate in the Firetrees. And he has an army of thuggish servants who could very well have snatched her for him. We've had officers surveying the place, but it's so built up with walls and spikes we can't see anything and have no evidence. But if that's so we'll find out—and find a way to bring her out. But I could believe Horrocks has gone to his father."

"Who calls him a bastard? Perhaps he simply ran away, no, he'd never do that … or else the old man ran into trouble and sent for him."

"After all that happened?"

"He thinks: my father needs me! Maybe he loves me after all! Doesn't that sound right to you, Director?"

"I hope to God it isn't. I'd much rather think he got up enough daring to confront his father—only that would be dangerous too! But then, he might turn up in an hour and we'll feel foolish."

She and Natalya looked at each other. *Maybe.* "But he's been missing twelve hours," Natalya said.

Mbai said, "If he cut out his chip, that's real trouble." She sighed again. "I know now why Semdah wanted to keep an eye on him. That may have been Zakarian's last secret …"

There was a tapping on the glass door.

"Look!" Natalya said. Horrocks was standing there with a smile on his face that was—what? Rueful, ironic, or both.

Mbai shook her head. "So much for everything we worried about." She opened the door and said, "Hello!" in a tone that required an answer.

"Sorry I missed the meeting," Horrocks said. "I got a call from my mother's lawyers in Altamir."

"Nothing really serious, I hope," Natalya said.

"No, no bad news." He was calm, and showed none of the vulnerability she had become tired of, impatient with…

"I just wanted to have breakfast, and I'll meet you in our room."

He went off; Natalya and Mbai glanced at each other with raised brows, and Mbai said, "I'll see you in half an hour."

Natalya sighed and went back to her own cubicle.

A tap on the door. Without raising her head, she knew, simply *knew* that Horrocks was on the other side. A deep breath. She touched the button, the door slid. Horrocks said, "I don't really want breakfast, and I'm sorry for bothering you, but I need to talk to you alone just one more time."

Natalya did her best to hide the sigh of resignation, and they went back to that little room with the nothing-colored walls and sat down in the worn chairs.

Horrocks put his hands on his knees and said, "I was called to Altamir to meet with my mother's lawyers. I presumed it was all about the will. She hadn't needed money, she kept working until she died, and there was still most of the money Vanbrennan had settled on her when I was born. No other heirs, no complications. But." He twisted in his chair and visibly tried to calm himself. "She'd left a sealed document that had to be opened in my presence. It had a long list of witnesses' signatures, it was written in her hand, and it said that I was not Henrik Vanbrennan's son and had no relationship to him whatever—"

Natalya was surprised to find herself relieved.

"—and there was not and never had been a person named Derek Vanbrennan. My mother had claimed she registered the name but did not—all the time I was growing up she called me Derek—imagine it! I don't want to know how she faked up the DNA."

Natalya shook her head.

Horrocks, still amazed, said, "Derek Vanbrennan doesn't exist and I don't miss him!"

Natalya said quietly, "I'm sorry for your mother."

"Yes … She was an intelligent woman, a good doctor, and she loved me … wonderful with children. But to adults she wasn't attractive or graceful, didn't quite know how to behave … and she so much wanted an ordinary family—God!—that she was ready to lie and cheat. My father— no, I mean Vanbrennan, hard to break the habit—he wanted an ordinary family with a Meshar woman!" He stopped and hung his head. "He called me a bastard, and I knew I was born out of wedlock. I guess what he really meant was that I wasn't his bastard. And oh my God, if he was the one who destroyed the project—whoever my real father was, he couldn't be worse than that … and all that love wasted."

"No, Horrocks. If you hadn't loved, your life would have been truly unbearable."

They sat silent, looking into the corners of the room without seeing them.

"I told the lawyers to send copies of her letter to Mbai and Semdah, and direct them to destroy it after they read it. I'm telling them I'll resign my position because I'm not working under false pretences—"

"Surely they wouldn't let you go!"

"Maybe not … but I certainly am glad I never told any of my women friends about being the son of the wealthy and famous Vanbrennan!"

"You'd better hurry off and choose the best of them and get yourself married, Horrocks. You really do need a family."

"Spoken like a mother. I know I've been a terrible annoyance, but I'm so relieved now that he isn't my father. And—and I'm so grateful for your help and patience. If you weren't married already I'd marry you!"

"Thank you very much!" Natalya stood up, blushing slightly. Her comm chimed then, and she welcomed the excuse to leave, but the voice that greeted her answer brought a message of dread.

SHAR: CAPITAL CITY:
ONE MORE DAY

Still another night to pass in the stone room. Jacko brought out his old scuffed pack of cards, dealt a hand of Wall-Eyed Stud, and scattered a packet of expired antibiotic pills for chips. He won most of the games, having been PanGalactic Poker King for seven seasons running.

Delius fell asleep thinking of old Arvig and his pain, and of his own son James doing his best to be brave about his father's leaving for far worlds…

꿍

He faced the world of Shar once more in that Council Hall. The Councillors were subdued and perhaps weary of discussion that droned on and seemed to go nowhere.

Arvig, pushing his life through the cloud of pain, took one more deep breath and said to Delius, "You have remained here these days, watching and listening. Now you can see what you are dealing with."

"A world of people who need help," Delius said. "I'd be lying if I let you believe we could restore the huge numbers of women the world needs, within the lifetime of even the youngest of your children. That will take multiple octads of years. There will be plenty of time for those who don't want women to change their minds or live peacefully without them—but the peaceful part will take a long time and much work. What people think they want so much may not look as good to them when they find out how very much work there is."

There was some murmuring in the background, but Arvig said mildly, "They already know quite a deal about the hard work. They learned it in the Mother-Halls."

Delius was properly humbled. "You are right, and I meant no insult. I myself hardly know how much can be done and how soon, considering our experience so far. But Galactic Federation will keep working at it, if you want it done."

"I have already admitted that your Federation has saved my life, as well as helping everyone else on the world stay alive."

Delius broke out in a sweat of hope. Aesh was free. The child Shemesh was restored. The symbols of restoration were preserved. "In that case we understand each other well. Then may I believe that you have decided to let us go on with our work for your world? Considering your strong relationship with the Polar Monarchies, and as far as I can tell with most other states, may we agree that you will allow us to begin?"

Arvig said resignedly, "That question must be finally decided by my Council." He spread his arms to include the thirty-eight: "Say now!"

It was Givor who spoke first, in a curiously moderate tone of voice: He had also been dealt his ration of pain from Ayin. "I would agree if I was sure that those who do not wish to change are not considered criminal."

"I have said so, and the right to choose will become an Act of Law."

Then various discussions broke out among twos and threes; they were heated but not violent, and Arvig simply sat down on his bench and let them range over the yeses, noes and maybes. He looked weary, but he had lost some of his tenseness.

Delius too had no more words to say. When the discussion began losing its decibels, he saw that his own work was nearly done.

Then there was a clattering at the gate and the guards stiffened.

A high voice cried out: "Where's Delius! Is Delius there?"

Delius's scalp began to prickle.

Arvig slammed the table with both fists. "What is it now! Have we not had enough barging in? Angry-God is surely twisting my tail!"

The voice called again, "For God's sake Delius, make them let me in!"

Cobb. The eccentric biologist. "That's one of my party, Arvig-lord. Please let him in."

Arvig gestured and a guard ran to open the gate.

"Delius!" Cobb cried hoarsely and rushed forward across the courtyard, stamping in his muddy boots, half-staggering, rips in his clothes, twigs in his hair, dirt on his face, his eyes darkened, burnt out with exhaustion and looking quite mad. At each elbow a Shar was holding him up, both of them dirt-splattered as well—

Delius gaped. "What!"

"This is what I call my lusus naturae!" In his bruised hands he was holding a rag-wrapped bundle. He controlled himself, slowed his steps and cleared his throat. "A gift, Arvig-lord!" Arvig gaped at him.

Cobb stretched out his arms to lay down the bundle and guards surrounded him.

"No, no, it's—"

The bundle yelped.

It seemed to Delius as if everyone in the world jumped.

The Councillors rose as one and crowded to look.

Cobb whispered, "Nothing dangerous now, it may one day be dangerous, but right now it won't bite you…"

"Animal?" Arvig murmured. "No…"

"Let me show you," Cobb said, still whispering. The bundle whimpered. He unwrapped it breathlessly as if it might be a treasure of diamonds, lifted it and held it up.

"I've seen everything a satellite has ever recorded here, and I've been looking for this for a very long time. My 'lusus naturae'."

It was a baby, crusted with dirt, slobber and feces, trembling, beginning to squall now. A female, according to the three red buds of its teats and the quivering arrow tip of its tail. Her left leg ended at the ankle.

Though she was missing a foot, and, to Delius's filtered nose, smelt of nothing but her own effluents, mud and rotting soil elements: though she was as far from the sweet clove scent of Shar people as their world is from all of the Twelveworlds or any other, to all those around her, Shar or Earthers, it seemed as if she had been born in an explosion of pheromones. A burst of female presence.

And a burst of murmuring among the Councillors.

Arvig had been holding his breath and now said, "It is a female…" As if his subjects had needed to be told.

Cobb said proudly, "She's not that good to look at, but there's a good hope of living with her, at least. Better than no head."

Delius asked, "Where did you find her?"

"In the Western Declivity. Unexplored, really, just like those islands where the Meshar bred true because they were isolated. With all the aboriginals in the caves out there, you can't see what's happening inside them, but they make their fires outside."

"She has a faint burned smell to her," Arvig said.

"Yes, I caught her just as they were putting her on the fire."

"What? They would eat her?"

"No, they're just a wild lot that make sacrifices to Angry-God. The missing foot, you find weird things in small populations. Like among the Meshar that live on Barrazan Five. I don't know whether the ones here pick these to sacrifice because of the disability or they just don't like females. But they're not the first tribe that'll sacrifice new people to old gods."

Delius made a deep obeisance to Arvig and said, "I beg that you allow Aesh son of Ohr to see this child."

Arvig looked hard at him with those red-black black-red eyes and said, "I will think about that. In the meantime, one of you caretakers out there, bring me the washing bowl and water jug from my tower, and also the comb."

A servant ran up and brought them down.

Delius with his crew and Cobb, watched as Arvig filled the bowl, dipped the rag in it and ran the water over the quivering baby once, twice, and three times, draining and refilling, combing, drying off, combing again until it became a child of the Shar, not merely a filthy lump of life. Then he wrapped it in a cloth and held it out to Delius, as Aesh had offered him the newborn Shemesh.

Delius clasped it, this tiny demonic creature in its dark and scraggy fur, with its pointed ears, arrow tail and female emblems, as if it had been his own. As he had done with Shemesh. The hope of her people, missing only a foot. He smiled and offered it back to Cobb, who grinned and said, "No, she needs cleaner hands now!" Then he nodded and ran off.

Arvig said mildly, "Does he not care for our company?"

"I expect he's gone off to look for more of them," Delius said. "But he'd better take care. He looked as if they did their best to tear him apart the first time."

"And he should look for their mothers, also, to find if they can breed true," Arvig said.

As Delius tendered back the child he saw Arvig raise his head and stare.

The Chief of Guards was escorting Aesh into the Council Chamber.

He bowed to Arvig and sidled off, leaving Aesh, who for that moment looked defenseless. Arvig set the child on the table and moved away.

Without being invited, Aesh came forward boldly enough. Delius moved aside for him. Carefully, Aesh extended his hand and cupped the stump of the tiny leg in his palm for a moment. Then he let go and stepped back.

Almost in outrage, Arvig cried out, "You have nothing to say?"

Aesh said quietly, "A beginning. I'm happy to see her." He turned and left the hall.

The baby began to squeal. Arvig picked it up and said, "We need a feeder for this one. Just like all the others." He added somberly, "And a Mother-Hall of her own."

Yes, and defense against all of those Shar who hated the project of restoring women. Again, Delius was struck with the terrible thought— the dream flashed in his mind—of Angry-God's creation of Unwoman.

True enough, that all who were born on this world suckled on the teats of Unwoman. And the first generation of true women would be grown in their bellies. Delius sighed. *So Arvig lost his son, and we gave him a daughter with a foot missing.*

And we don't know if this one will open her eyes, and listen and speak.

But even so, Arvig was glad to have that much.

ᵂᵂ

"Yeh, one deactivated male gene, and so far we're not sure of mending it…" Cobb was weary from his searches, grateful for being invited to bunk with Delius and his crew rather than in one of the mining shacks where he usually slept. "The team on your world did their best, but we're just beginning here, and you know, there's never been a Genome Project for the Shar. With this little one right here on the world, we can hope. Her presence tells us that her father is genetically healthier than most male

Shar, except, of course, for the matter of that missing foot. We can also find out what her genome has to tell us—and her womb-bearer's. If we can find a whole one, it will still be a long while before we can harvest eggs—even from embryonic cells.

"But we can start planning to tame those fellows down in the Declivity enough to get samples from them, and the Shar people will have to gather a force that can stop them from sacrificing to Angry-God … old Arvig has a lot more persuading to do. And needs much more time to do it … There's a lot to think about, trying to grow this shrinking population. Increasing food production first."

"That's one more big problem," Delius said.

"I could've gone down there years ago and maybe saved more females, but my department didn't have the funds to send me until the deal with Xanthrotek, and your project manager decided to spend some of the money on me."

"I expect they'll find more of it now."

"Possibly, if the mines keep giving and our sponsor—" looking upward, "—too. If that big demolition didn't put them off track altogether—it was supposed to be kept secret, but I heard about it from more than one source, and it took a hearty bite of their income. Here, we were given a piece of luck with this baby. It doesn't happen often, but sometimes evolution takes thought and backs up a bit."

Mick said, "I don't expect we'll see chimpanzees in the maternity wards, do you?"

Cobb laughed. "We'd have to go pretty far back on the branch for that … I realize we won't get to see anything near the end of it, Delius, and neither will these poor juddars in all their hundreds of thousands. They'll need a big crew of specialists who have more experience than I do."

"Maybe at least they'll know where to begin," Delius said.

"Eh, but in a way we've done a sampling of what we wanted to do with that exploded project: produce a female. That's some kind of beginning. Anyway, I want to call it one."

☙❧

Mick and Jacko rolled into their bedding but Cobb and Delius were still wakeful from the day's work.

"Now your time is up here, Delius," Cobb said. "You did a lot in a short while, just getting them to agree to accept help, and you'll be able to hitch onto the *Zarandu*."

Then Angry-God forced words out of Delius's mouth:

"But in the end, all that we're doing, congratulating ourselves, what good will it do them, all those years away?" He froze, shocked at finding himself thinking in this way.

Cobb squeezed his flaming brows together. But he spoke quietly. "First, a few more females and even more coming will give them enough hope to keep them alive. And after that, it'll give them another point of view about our people—you've managed a deal of that already—and us too!" He laughed. "Do you regret all the work you've done on all those worlds?"

"I haven't done all that much here. I've saved Aesh's skin but I've left him without anything else."

"He's alive. Everything else is beyond your power."

"True enough. I'm just tired, and resentful of having this project pushed on me." Delius took a long breath and rubbed his eyes.

"I've been there, Delius, believe me, but this one I've been waiting for all my life."

FTHEL IV:

NATALYA IN DEEP

The scar tingled with what felt like electrical charges up and down Natalya's neck and she could not stop the shaking deep under her breast-bone. She hurried to Mukherjee's office.

"What?"

His mild smile greeted her, and she swallowed the lump in her throat and forced out words. "I—I thought Levona looked as if she'd become pregnant—" she spat the word as if it was on fire, "everything being so disorganized here—my God I don't know how I could have been so stupid being happy they'd made friends! I had her called into the Hospital. And now Gynecology tells me she—she's bearing twins, females, but one of them—one of them…"

His eyes lit up. "Is one of *them?*"

She felt her jaw dropping. "You're happy about this?"

"If the two of them stay alive, if one of them is whole—"

"But I should have taken care—"

"If it works out it's one more for the population and one for the research. We need them. At the least it shows that our work on the male genome had some effect."

"But I was wrong to give those two so much freedom. Mbai will be furious, and Levona will be horrified to bear that…"

"Mbai is not your superior, nor mine neither, and I will take care of her. Levona won't need to be responsible for either of these. And so far neither of them is born. Is Levona upset?"

"According to records, she bore two healthy children on her home world, and she doesn't seem bothered. I guess she takes it as a matter of course." She sighed. "I wish I could. Of course she doesn't know of…"

Mukherjee touched her shoulder gently, "On Barrazan Five they live in mixed groups and take what comes. If we're lucky enough to have these alive, we'll learn. And we truly need to do that. I've just heard that my friend Cobb discovered a newborn female in an area of Shar that hadn't been much explored. It has the Meshar mutation but I welcome it."

"I only hope one of these is whole."

"When are they due?"

"They're about half way, around three thirtydays."

"We'll keep watch—on her and the other two women."

Natalya hurried back to her own office, where she darkened the glass, flicked on the lights, and scratched around in her desk drawers to find a squirt of Axodyne (a product of Xanthrotek, like all other medications here) for her headache. She was grateful that her office had no room for more than one. One person, one headache.

☜☞

Two days later Mukherjee called on her, and said, "I don't know whether this will make you feel better or worse."

"What is it?"

"About Levona, the abnormal fetus has miscarried."

"And the other?"

"It seems to be normal," he said. "It's nerve-wracking waiting to find out."

"Genetic flaws…"

"Maybe," Mukherjee said. "But I'm told Meshar have almost never had twins. There may simply not be enough room in the uterus, and the weaker one was forced out. We have enough fetal tissue to examine, but I wish we'd had all of it."

"For Levona's sake, I don't."

* * T H I R T E E N * *

A PLACE AT THE TABLE

For one last time Delius was welcomed and sat down at Arvig's table with his thirty-nine Councillors.

"We will wait for one more," Arvig said.

Delius wondered if he was referring to Ayin, but no, that would be impossible after what had happened. And the pain was ebbing from Arvig's face and body language.

Delius was not quite surprised when Aesh came to sit at the empty place. "I am very glad to see you here," he said in Aesh's own Northern dialect.

"I am glad to be here," Aesh said in the same mother tongue, and then less formally, "I am not going to campaign for the Emperor's place."

"You are welcome to do so for a place on the Council," Arvig said. There was a quietness around the table; it gave off no hostility, only the sense of waiting.

Aesh cocked his head. "If you think I can stop up my mouth." There was an awkward silence.

But Arvig said, "Truth may hurt, but still it must be spoken."

No one answered.

Delius felt deeply relieved. Then he said carefully, "I want to go home believing that I have offered the support of Galactic Federation and that you are of a mind to accept it." He found this statement difficult to express in the local dialect and repeated it in *lingua*. He waited for the reaction, but there was none.

Arvig said, "I have already accepted. I promise, and I will swear on the Stone if you choose."

"You needn't. I am content to have your promise."

And Delius closed his eyes for a moment. *Home now.*

He took a deep breath, and said, "It will be difficult. Aesh-lord was right when he advised talking quietly. You need more members for Galactic Federation in the orbits and on the ground. The stronger you become the more greedy people there will be trying to keep you down. I will do my best to help you but I have very little power."

"You have helped," Arvig said, "and this session will close the archive."

As the meeting broke up, Arvig gestured at Delius to sit down again. "I must speak to you."

Delius sat and waited, uneasily, as Arvig worked at moistening his mouth.

"My son Ayin has confessed," Arvig said at last. "To all the evil that he did."

Delius said quickly, "You needn't tell me." He did not like to think of how Ayin might have been made to confess.

"I need to tell you," Arvig said. "He was so determined that he or Givor or both would take control of this Council, he found that Shar you saw die horribly, that son of the Angry-God who would do his filthy work, and he bribed him to kill our orbit's Representative Dos Ramos as well as Aesh, son of Ohr, and—and me, if necessary."

"I believed that was the case."

"For once the Angry-God was stopped." Arvig wetted his lips again.

"Aesh and I were saved. I should be making this confession of mine to Aesh," he said bitterly. He was trembling.

"You were mistaken, but you did nothing evil," Delius said, deeply embarrassed. "That should be the end of it."

"Yes, it should." Arvig took a deep breath. "You are free to go home now. Good life to you then, Observer."

EXITS

FTHEL IV:

RUAH AND VANBRENNAN AND ...

No one took her—or let her go—out of the strange room where the dead one was kept, except to the lavatory, and there she was watched with cold uninterest. She began to wish she was as dead as the woman in the box. Sometimes when the old man left the room at mealtimes the servants jeered at her, but did not dare touch her. But Vanbrennan paid less attention to her now, and shut himself away in rooms she had never seen. Her food was served in a bowl on one of the small tables. Sometimes he watched her eat— it seemed to her, as she had watched animals and insects eating at home on Barrazan Five: with distant curiosity.

The days passed, and she closed her eyes to remember Barrazan, the storms and their lightning flashes on that world. She did not know whether the drug that kept her from shifting would cripple her forever, but she forced herself to believe that there was freedom somewhere, alive or dead.

Anger burned out of her like fire.

᠀ ᠀

In the evenings the vast room with its hangings of woven stuff on the walls, alternating with flashing mirrors, and between them trumpet-shaped sconces holding lights that looked and flickered like flames but were not fire; the windows of all possible shapes and sizes with colored transparent panes, and the soft floors of swirling patterns, red, green, blue, the chairs, benches, tables that in the half-light seemed transformed into the tortured shapes of alien bodies with writhing legs, bearing strange objects just as twisted and without meaning—all these swarmed around her and that dead one she was meant to replace, creating only dizziness.

And the beings here now, the ones from the camp who had brought her here, with their bristled heads and jaws, squatting on the floor. Sometimes rising to bring drinks and bits of food to the unsmiling old man on his throne. His wrinkles deepened in the shadowy light, and he reminded her of old shrunk men of the Meshar, their wits lost to age, who hunched on the ground and scratched at the soil as if it would feed them.

Women began to come in, some who had brought food to her, some who worked in other parts of this mansion and never appeared here. They were dressed in strips of cloth that showed naked flesh swelling between them, such nakedness as she had never seen before; she wondered that they would leave themselves so vulnerable and her guardhairs rose at the thought.

But then there was reason enough for her hairs to rise. There was nothing to show that the old beast wouldn't kill her quickly if she fought, no matter how savage her anger, and she sensed some difference in him tonight undefined, and morbid. He could never beget any child now, this man so old, and he was tired of playing with her. She crouched tightly as if she were about to spring, tail curved back of her for balance and hands half clenched, glistening with the red veins in their claws.

Vanbrennan reached over and pulled at one of her wrists and in her attempt to twist away she noticed for the first time that the casket, the old

Meshar woman's last prison, was empty. "I have something special for you tonight," he told his guests.

The lamps dimmed to near darkness.

In one of the walls was a great screen that projected depictions of whatever Vanbrennan felt like looking at: sometimes only the same patterns as the floor covering, sometimes a starry night, or a blazing fire on logs. Mainly a performance by naked aliens of half-a-score species writhing in a mass of limbs to throbbing music with lightning cracks and echoes of thunder in it.

Occasionally they jumped out of the screen as holograms to enact their savage loves among the watchers.

These always frightened Ruah, and she knew the old man enjoyed her dizziness and terror: emblems of his power. But then he had never said he loved her or anything else except to tell her of his jealousy and hatred.

The visionary figures flashed and twisted, and the watchers grabbed at each other and began to ape them. Shadows grew around them and the music ebbed. The grunting watchers realized its fading and pulled away in a sweat, snorting. *Give us some more! Give us more!*

Vanbrennan watched with an expressionless face, as if he were pulling himself away from all of them, and Ruah waited for him to release her wrist, but he did not.

The music stopped and the screen whitened. In the center of it the image of a small walking figure appeared, coming forward and growing larger. He was a short, slightly pudgy man. Though his hair was carefully combed and parted, his clothes were shabby, a wrinkled shirt, worn and ragged jeans and scuffed white shoes. There was the merest glint of a small silver cross on a chain around his neck.

Vanbrennan, startled, bent forward. "What's this! I never ordered this! Turn it off!"

The figure said, "You can't turn me off, Vanbrennan."

Vanbrennan cried out in a high raveled voice, "Who are you and what do you want?"

The men and women around him were catcalling and yelling, "Get him off! What's he on there for? Give us more of the good stuff!"

"My name is Zakarian," the image said in a cold quiet voice. "I know everything about you, Henrik Vanbrennan, and I have told it to everyone who will listen. Most all, the authorities.

"I know that three years ago you sold four fifths of your holdings in Xanthrotek to three mining companies. Yes, I know that was not against the law, and I have ways of finding out. Then a tenday after that sale the Shar experiment blew up, the project was forced to stop, and the value of that company shrank."

"That had nothing to do with me!" Vanbrennan yelled.

"Your company gave a part of the funds for the hospital wing, fair enough, and some of your employees worked on the building, easy reach for planting explosives."

"It's lies, all lies!"

Zakarian the image stepped out of the screen as a hologram. Blurring slightly first, then clearing and stark. As if he were growing out of the carpeted floor.

"That kidnapped Meshar woman you brought here from Barrzan Five, the one we couldn't save, died and you wanted another, and you were planning to pick one out of the hospital wing, but there was this one right here, outside and running loose.

"That scruffy camp in Bonzador state that thought they were going to steal a ship and attack a world, where she went for safety because she didn't know any better, you had a man in there and he drove her to *shift* out to someone you had waiting. He caught her and delivered her to you, and that man you left in the camp you never bothered taking out, so when the police were swarming and breaking the place up, they took hold of him and he told them everything to save himself, when you wouldn't save him."

"That's nothing but lies!" Vanbrennan burst with sweat, and seemed to shrink from loss of water.

"Then you got tired or bored, or both. Or just too old. And not long ago you sold this estate, didn't you, and bought a one-way ticket, just one, shipping off alone to the other side of the world, and maybe offworld from there. Going to say goodbye to all your friends? Or sell them?"

The men and women around Ruah and Vanbrennan began to move away from them, men first and then the women crawling and stumbling their way toward the walls and their exits.

They left Ruah and Vanbrennan alone in the circle of space.

Vanbrennan opened his mouth like a beast and cried out in a harsh voice, "If you want her alive you and your forces back out of here."

He raised his other hand, the blade of a knife flickered through the dusk like lightning pointed at Ruah.

The stoked fire in her spirit flamed.

In one sweep she bent down and sank her fangs into his grasping fist until they gritted on the knucklebones.

He screamed and

*

she was on hands and knees on the floor of a wide hall lined with stairways and balconies on one side and on the other, multicolored glass windows that rose so high she could not see the ceiling. She had no tunic or clogs. Or any of the anti*shift* drug in her either, evidently. She spat Vanbrennan's blood.

An Earther woman was walking toward her. She was dressed in a green uniform with a gold badge on one shoulder, an official of some kind.

Ruah pulled back crouching and saw a tall bony man with rust-colored hair following after, and then a burst of other uniformed officers with guns who swarmed around her grunting and sweating, calling out, "They're inside that room, that's where they are, watch out for knives!" They fired shots in the air and began breaking through the doors.

She and the two others were left in the hall.

She recognized Horrocks, the man from the hospital. He was running toward her now, but she was trembling and could not move. She knew again the savage mix of anger, pleasure and guilt that had first gripped her when she attacked those tramps in the woodlands, it shortened her breath.

Horrocks and the Earther woman pulled her to her feet. "I'm so glad to find you, Ruah! This officer will take you back to the hospital."

She growled, unable to stop panting, "I want to be free, I want home."

"We'll do our best to do that for you," Horrocks said, in her dialect. "I promise."

"Promises are made but not kept," she said bitterly.

"Then I swear."

DELIUS, HOMEWARD BOUND FROM SHAR

Aesh said: "I feel now that a Councillor has more of a voice than I had as an emperor. Emperors have no greater voice because they are always obeying the demands of the suppliers and defending themselves against the criticisms of the Councillors—ayeh! I should never admit such things to you!"

"I won't tell anyone."

"I know you will not. I know also that Arvig-lord was meaning to console me for being unjustly accused. I suppose I am doing my best to console myself."

Aesh and Delius were sitting on benches in Kohav's small house, while Shemesh squatted on the floor playing a game of sticks and stones.

Kohav and Sefer were out back raking up soil for a kitchen garden.

Delius said, "As long as the Federation is allowed to support your people it will give more strength and independence to the Council."

"And some for myself! At least I have the power to help Kohav bring a complaint against that neighbor who bakes the stinking dirtweed in his coalpot and the other one who plays the nose flute all night." With his head cocked to one side, Aesh was not speaking with gravity, and Delius was pleased to see this spark in him. "And I have hired Kohav as my aide."

"You will live here in this house, will you?"

"For now. My father would prefer that I live with him, but as much as I respect him, I'm closer to him with some space between us…" He thought for a moment, and said, "We Shar are such a small people, and there is so much work to be done."

Delius stood. "True enough, and both the Federation and the Council are lucky to have you working for us. We'll keep our promises." Delius was not one to cross his fingers.

"It is good to have known you, Aesh Seven," he said, and bowed, as he had done to the Emperor Aesh Seven, then left.

ORBIT

Once again in the orbit, Delius was forced to wait in the station for Mick and Jacko because, as before, there had been no space for them. The place was a square room lined in some kind of dirty white plastic tile, with one wall arching upward, and he shared the space with twenty-odd others, a few of them women who were not at all like the fresh youthful ones he had met earlier on the way down.

He looked out through the oval windows at the world crackling with lightning on its dark side, shrouded in dusty clouds over most of its surface, and wondered how he could tell himself that the journey had in any way improved the conditions for its people.

But Cobb had found his "lusus naturae", that whole, or almost whole female who was so rare as to be a freak. Cobb and Arvig and most of the Councillors—at least for the moment—would believe that even keeping the Shar from each other's throats over the effort to restore women was an achievement. Delius had come to this world for that purpose, and if the peace was kept…

Every few moments through a break in the clouds he could see a flash like a jewel on the world's surface, and knew it was one or another of the steel gates, like clenched fangs, guarding the adyts of the mines inside, as if some poor fool might want to crawl in and steal its stones.

Of the others with him, there were three or four species mixed with the Earthers; some of the Bengtvadi were managers of the crews that operated the robot miners, and most of the blue Varvani were crew members, all going for a change of working conditions—the equivalent of health leave—either on the *Zarandu* or the *Aleksandr Nevskii II*. Like Delius, they were dressed in safe-suits that had seen much wear, and the Earthers were a worn down red-faced lot, mainly, who did a deal of coughing and nose-blowing in the thick musty air and threw their well-used nose filters on the floor. They were tired from their rounds of work and had not much more to say than how glad they were to be off-world.

"A shit pit if ever was one."

Delius found a pull-down seat at the wall and closed his eyes.

Something poked him.

A dirty finger. One of the red faces was glaring at him. "Hey, you one of them GalFedders?"

He said with careful sleepiness, "That's who I work for."

A sneer. "You been trying to train the animals down there?"

"I was trying to help the people."

"What are we supposed to help them for? They ain't no people!"

"They are according to Galactic Federation."

"Our companies pay GalFed for nothing!"

"Your companies get a lot off this world, so you're giving something back."

"But them there's just animals that ought to be in cages. They'll tear you apart if you look at them."

More voices joined in. "Yah! You even seen any what-they-call females?"

"I've seen them."

"And don't they make you want to puke?"

"They make me sorry that they can't enjoy their lives or their children. They don't get in your way, or make your lives harder."

"Listen to him, you hear that? He don't have to grub in dirt, he gets to stay nice and clean, he's got it easy!"

Delius felt the stir of resentment around him, an old familiar feeling. He was beginning to wonder if it had been by chance that he was here without Mick and Jacko. "You think so? I came here because I'm an Observer. GalFed Surveyors tell me about dangerous conditions on a world, so I go alone to the colony where settlers are living comfortably in peace and tell them the mountain-side they've built their homes on is going to be covered in lava before they know it, and they have to move or die."

"Just like that?"

"No. I tell them what the Federation will do to help them move. If they're lucky it'll be some other part of the same world. But they can't stay."

"Who pays for it?"

"Whatever branch of the Federation put them there."

"You really go alone?"

"Most of the time, so people know I'm not threatening."

"They ever try to kill you?" An eager voice.

"Enough times. I've done some rolling in the dirt, but I fought them off. I know how to fight." His cold stone father had seen to that, and when he grew tall enough Delius had taught him a few things in return. "Now that I have a wife and kid, I bring a couple of helpers."

One last voice asked, "But you always get to save them?"

"No. Not always."

Mick and Jacko opened the door at this moment, so there was no need to flex the iron bar of an arm and more. The two came in, nodded, and squatted in corners. Delius leaned back and closed his eyes.

He was not angry at these workers. They no longer dug in the mines to have the grit worked into their skin or the roof caving in over them, but struggling with the thick safety-suits, stifling heat, and massive robots that took all their strength to control, they deserved all the risk pay their unions battled for.

When he rose to leave, a foot shot out to trip him. He had been expecting something like that and gave it a hard kick in the ankle, not to let that bunch off too easy.

❧

In seven standard hours he was accepting the injection of coldsleep, sinking into the half-death, the only road home.

* * F O U R T E E N * *

FTHEL IV:

AN INTERLUDE WITH SEMDAH

Delius had much to catch up on, but the Department took mercy on him and gave him to his family for a day.

In bed that night, one flesh with Natalya, Delius said, "That's it. I'm home and I'm staying home."

"Ssh," Natalya said. "You're here now."

"I wonder what will happen with Aesh." About to tip over the edge of sleep, but with his mind still boiling, he murmured, "There's a very old story, myth I suppose, that the first Aesh was born out of an Earther woman's body."

Natalya sniffed, "Um, I think that's a story I'd rather not know."

"I'll bet old Vanbrennan knew it—and believed it."

"Sleep."

⸙

At breakfast next morning, Natalya told him of Vanbrennan's arrest, Horrocks's disillusionment, and Zakarian's reappearance. A long summing-up.

"That is good. But I always found it hard to believe he had died," Delius said.

James, at the beginning of a growth spurt now, a measure of the time he'd been gone, stuck to him like glue, so Delius took him to the hive and squeezed him into the cubicle alongside himself. Genever caught sight of him. "Hullo, Delius, good to have you back."

"Good to be back." Yes, even Genever's overdone smoothness was a genuine welcome home.

Horrocks knocked on his door. "Hello, Delius, you made it!"

"And what good luck hit on you, Horrocks?"

Horrocks was grinning, the first time Delius had ever seen him smile. "Vishniak's retiring and I've applied to be an Oberver on Barrazan Five— no, not for the Meshar women, and no, I won't try to find a wife there, I'm getting married to a young woman I knew when I was a student, that neither my mother nor my false father approved of."

"I guess you've graduated then, Horrocks."

Mbai, amazingly, visited him at his cell in the hive rather than summoning him to her own. "You don't look a day older, Delius."

"I heard about Zakarian."

"Yes, and we've had a fine healthy female Shar born to us in the hospital, and Horrocks is going out to work with Kogol and Vishniak on Barrazan Five and taking that woman Ruah—oh, there's a deal of news and gossip you'll be hearing. And Semdah will be expecting you in a quarter hour."

ܐ܀ܐ

Semdah was not one for effusive greetings.

"I hope you are not still angry with me, Delius."

"How could I be? You told me you would guard my family with your life."

"I would have done, if need be."

"I believed you."

"But I was not happy endangering you, Delius. I sent you there because our friend Cobb told us it was possible that at least a few normal females could be found on Shar if one knew where to look for them. I felt that your empathy with Aesh and other Shar would keep their Council from falling apart and giving up what they needed so badly, and Cobb would have the opportunity to search. I found funds for him because he wasn't getting enough from his own department. And as for Zakarian, I am sorry for deceiving you. I told you lies, and insulted him as well, to shield him.

"I trusted that Zakarian knew everything. I always have done, as long as I've known him, and I'm not even sure why. He came to me with the suspicion that Vanbrennan had engineered the destruction of the project and I gave him the authority to investigate and act on it. He gave up all his possessions to stage that 'death'. Yes, and we are going to renew that project, Delius, no matter how hard we have to wring those orbiting companies and our Federation to squeeze the funds out of them." She nodded grimly, and added, "There are many things I want to change in the way we operate. We need institutions built on the world, so we don't have to breed females here and ship them out. We need to be able to teach the Shar to grow and breed more of their food, build stronger houses, forge metals, keep dirt out of the air. We also need a great number of people who agree with my ideas. All of that will take a huge wealth of funds and a great many of Shar's octads of years. I'll be dead long before all that comes to pass, but no matter.

"And Zakarian will be paid too." She twisted her face into one of those particularly primate expressions. "I have not forgotten the risk pay you were promised … and about your own future, Delius, that has to be decided, but not in any hurry."

Delius would not argue with that.

BARRAZAN V:
R U A H

It was a repeat, in a way, of that visit long ago. Surely it was for Horrocks, coming down the stairs into the remnant of the old Station under the stormy heavens of the savage world. His hand was on Ruah's shoulder, lightly placed to warn off hostility. For Ruah was fearful.

Vishniak and Kogol were waiting for them, with a group of members from the clans' councils, all tense. They were crouched together in that bowl, the children among them hushed to quietness by the serious mien of their parents.

One of the clan leaders, an older woman of dignified presence, said, "Where are all the others? Is it true that they are dead?"

"Three are dead, killed by an evil person who has been found and is being punished," Horrocks said. "The rest are in good health, and one has had a child, a whole one. Ruah has helped us very much in catching that evil one, and I have brought her home to you. Your Observer Vishniak here, would like to go to his home, and I am staying in his place. We will also bring other people here, as soon as we can, to help you have more children, and healthier ones."

Horrocks watched them cautiously, having just casually committed a lot of funds that he hoped could be raised, but no one had anything to say about the frightful birth of the unwoman that had so horrified the Meshar. And been most likely dealt with. Still, something to watch out for. But not today.

Another of the leaders addressed Ruah: "Now that you have done all this good, as this one says, do you think you are better than all of us?"

"I do not," Ruah said firmly, "but I am as good as anyone here or anywhere."

"She sounds like herself," the old woman said, "so sit down with us now, Ruah, and share our dinner."

"No, no," Zakarian said to Delius years later. He had new lodgings, his usual kind of minimal hideaway with even more equipment, and was wearing crisp and stylish clothes of linen and leather. Delius wondered if he was still living alone. "I moved out most of the electronics in good time. The awards and prizes stuff I didn't need."

"How did you manage all that?"

"I have friends in low places."

"Eh. But you took the money."

"Don't you think I earned it?"

Delius could not avoid thinking that Zakarian would feel some perverse triumph at destroying all of those gifts awarded by "lesser minds".

"Yes, I guess you did earn it, when you could really have been killed. That was a horrible risk you took with the Meshar woman, Ruah."

"I had to. As soon as I found out that Vanbrennan had bought passage for one, I was sure he was tired of her—and for God's sake too damned old to beget anything!—so was meaning to kill her. The police had been hovering around him for a long while, I don't believe he could have dodged them for much longer, and I couldn't see him letting her go free. I was only trying to keep him talking until the police could break into the room. I didn't expect her to save herself."

"You're damned lucky she did."

"She's lucky too, don't forget."

"Whatever made you take on such a dangerous assignment?"

"It's a story, I guess. My father ran off early and my mother was an Observer on Barrazan Five, where Vishiak and Kogol were, where Horrocks is keeping an eye on the Meshar now. I was just a kid and I raised a big fuss when she left me with my old dried up aunt and uncle. So she gave me this cross," he touched it, "as a pledge that she'd never desert me." He cleared his throat.

"Vanbrennan was making his famous visit then, and when he took a fancy to that Meshar woman, of course she didn't want to leave, but he threw money at everybody, and threatened to cancel the deal with Xanthrotek ... my mother tried to save that Meshar, fought for her, but one day Vanbrennan just bundled her off ... and my mother disappeared. Like that. No investigation. No body. Nothing. And I was a kid, stuck with those old folks, they fed and clothed me, so I grew up." He lit a dopestick.

"Now, there was no way I could ever get a hold on the old bastard, but when Semdah gave me the chance, I took it."

"Do you think it's ever possible that he'd be charged for kidnapping?"

"No! Then there'd be a grip on all those who took his bribes. No. But he's in prison with enough charges that I don't think he'll come out alive."

But that discussion was years away.

FTHEL IV:
CITY OF ALTAMIR

Delius had nothing more to do on this evening than sit in the vast dining hall of a palatial hotel with a crystal goblet of vodka on ice and watch Natalya teaching James to dance, or at least doing her best. Her blue silk dress floated around her, an improvement on the sickly green of hospital gear.

He was spending his risk pay. Trying to live further beyond Shar and Meshar. But strangely, the space around him kept reminding him of the Birthing Center in the city called Equatorial Lands; the red evening sky beyond the windows might barely stand in for noon on Shar, the dignified servitors with their trays had a ceremonial look to them—he pulled himself away from the vision.

Something that had begun grandly with great ceremony had ended raggedly—or better, paused with a forward look of hard work and hope. That's what you get, Delius, Cobb would have said.

But Cobb had died working down in the Declivity, killed by Shar who were fiercely savage and did not want to give up their sacrificial victims. Over the years he had found and saved seven true females, six without blemish. Future egg producers. As Cobb would have wanted, his death did not stop the search for female Shar.

And Delius was content to wait for whatever task might demand his attention. Meanwhile Natalya, James, vodka on ice…

SHAR: CAPITAL CITY:
WISH

Life went on quietly. In Council Aesh spoke up when his voice needed to be heard, and no one complained. Councillors retired, new ones were voted in, Arvig died of old age. Some voices rose to say that Aesh should once again run for Emperor, but they were few and not loud.

Aesh did not encourage them. "What would I call myself then? Aesh Eight?" Among the other thirty-nine, some intelligent and mild-mannered substitute was found, who had a way of dealing with both the orbiters and Galactic Federation that improved conditions and intensified research.

Aesh had Kohav, Shemesh and Sefer for his family.

Gradually, Aesh became aware that something was disturbing Sefer to the point that he was pulling away from the others and barely taking part in conversations.

Aesh waited for an opportunity to be alone with him.

"What's troubling you, Sefer? Surely you can tell me after all these years."

Sefer was silent for a deep moment. He pulled his head down so that he seemed to shrink, and said finally, in a low voice, "I would like … I would like to have a child of my own."

The idea had never occurred to Aesh, and he was embarrassed to think that his world-view had been so limited by his sterility. He said thoughtfully, "If Kohav agrees, we could build another room on this house, and now that we've gotten rid of the dirtweed and the nose flute it would be good to have a new child's voice around here. If that's too hard on Kohav, we will find somewhere else."

Even if we have to live with my father. He'd bite his tongue before he would say that aloud.

"Do you truly mean that?"

"Truly I do!"

Sefer, filled with joy, said, "If it is a son I will share him with you, the way Kohav has done with Shemesh."

Aesh whispered, "If all goes well, perhaps it might even be a true daughter."

* * A U T H O R ' S   N O T E * *

When I first created the species "Shar" I kept unconsciously giving them Hebrew nouns for names. As I realized this I decided that the names seemed to fit, so I kept on doing it whenever the Shar turned up in my work. The names in this novel mean: Shar = gate; Ruah = breath/spirit; Aesh = fire; Ohr = light; Shemesh = sun; Kohav (kochov) = star; Levonah = moon, Bosor = meat.

* * A F T E R W O R D * *

by Nalo Hopkinson

The year was 1985. I was working as a clerk at Toronto's Fairview Public Library. I was re-shelving paperbacks when one of them caught my eye. From its cover I'd already pegged it as science fiction, my favorite genre. The cover depicted lionlike big cats in a futuristic landscape that they appeared to both own and have created. Its title was *The Kingdom of the Cats*. The "SF" label that the library had put on the spine confirmed the genre. But there was a second label on the spine; the little red maple leaf that signified that the book was by a Canadian author. That was my introduction to Phyllis Gotlieb, and to the "Starcats" series.

I had come to Canada as a teenager in the mid seventies, and the books that I was given in high school as emblematic of Canadian literature seemed to be overwhelmingly about winter and eternal existential solitude. It wasn't the books, some of which were excellent; it was a sameness of affect about that them that I suspect had more to do with which books were on the curriculum than with the actual breadth of Canadian literature. Up until the *The Kingdom of the Cats*, the only Canadian novels I'd seen that came anywhere near my beloved science fiction and fantasy were Margaret Atwood's *The Edible Woman* and Marian Engel's *Bear* (though I'm afraid that once I'd satisfied my curiosity by reading the infamous woman/bear sex scene in the latter novel, I didn't read much further). That was to be a banner year for me as far as Canadian science fiction was concerned. It was also the year that the first *Tesseracts* anthology of Canadian science fiction and fantasy appeared, edited by Judith Merril.

I took *The Kingdom of the Cats* home somewhat trepidatiously, fearing more of the same ilk of Canadian literature I'd read, except with aliens instead of humans.

I needn't have worried. It had plot. It had romance. It had murder and intrigue. It had sentient, telepathic, large red cats; what was not to love? I read the novel, enjoyed it, and made a mental note to look for more of Phyllis Gotlieb's work. Since then, I've read and enjoyed more of her novels and short stories, have had the honor of meeting her and hearing her speak, and have had the pleasure of being involved in the creation of the Sunburst, Canada's first juried award for Canadian literature of the fantastic, named after Phyllis's first published novel.

As my own political consciousness evolved, I began to appreciate Phyllis's understanding of how power plays out between and within cultures, and how it affects those on the wrong end of the power gradient, whether by virtue of gender, race, economics, class, or sexual orientation. Through the weave of layered, fraught, plots set in nonexistent places amongst aliens, both human and otherwise, Phyllis dissects the politics of power with clarity of insight, deftness of touch, and compassion. Often when I read a piece of her fiction, I come away with no binarized picture of a plucky hero pitted against a gloating villain. Phyllis possesses a keen understanding of the pressures experienced by people, any people, who try to buck the status quo to do what they see as right and necessary. Her characters have an appealing dignity and quirkiness to them. No clichés from Central Casting here, but relatable, flawed beings.

The leavening is love and humor. In *Flesh and Gold* and its sequel, *Violent Stars*, the Lyhhrt that so resolutely isolates itself from group mind connection with its people until it can accomplish a self-chosen task is one of the strangest aliens I've seen in this genre. Beings of the Lyhhrt race are small, shapeless blobs that get about by creating elaborate exoskeletons that they operate from within and that they alter or replace as needed; sort of like hermit crab meets caddis fly larva meets waldo. Every time I saw that sole, individuated Lyhhrt I wanted to giggle. But its whole race was so hell-bent on performing a selfless act of atonement for a great wrong of theirs that I couldn't help but be impressed by their dedication to the principle. And in *Birthstones*, Shar leader Aesh Seven knowingly risks his life and the trust of his people to shelter the son of his dear friend, Kohav. Phyllis's characters love so hard, and work so hard at rolling with the ironies that life throws at them, that one half falls in love with them oneself.

Phyllis Bloom was born in May 1926, and has been creating fiction and poetry amongst us for decades. I was at the party where she saw a published copy of *Flesh and Gold* for the first time. From the glee on her face when she saw that book, I knew that she is as passionate about her writing now as she's ever been. When I read *Flesh and Gold*, and now *Birthstones*, I knew that her voice and vision remain vital to this genre, and are a gift to us. In this her eightieth year, I'm thrilled to be able to congratulate her on *Birthstones*, her new novel. Mazel Tov, Phyllis! I'm a few months late to wish you "Happy Birthday," but for this at least, I'm on time.

* * R O B E R T   J .   S A W Y E R   B O O K S * *

Letters from the Flesh by Marcos Donnelly
Getting Near the End by Andrew Weiner
Rogue Harvest by Danita Maslan
The Engine of Recall by Karl Schroeder
A Small and Remarkable Life by Nick DiChario
Sailing Time's Ocean by Terence M. Green
Birthstones by Phyllis Gotlieb
The Commons by Matthew Hughes

And from Red Deer Press

Iterations by Robert J. Sawyer

www.robertjsawyerbooks.com

* * A B O U T   T H E   A U T H O R * *

As a poet, Phyllis Gotlieb has been nominated for Canada's highest literary honor, the Governor General's Award. As a science fiction writer, she has received a lifetime-achievement Canadian Science Fiction and Fantasy Award (the "Aurora") and been nominated for the Nebula Award. Canada's annual juried prize for fantastic literature, the Sunburst Award, is named after her first SF novel, *Sunburst*.

Phyllis's novels have been published by US science-fiction powerhouses Ace and Tor, and have been translated into Dutch, French, German, Italian, Japanese, and Norwegian. A fixture in Canadian science-fiction circles for four decades, she co-edited the second volume of the acclaimed *Tesseracts* anthology series and has written plays for CBC Radio. At its founding in 1965, she was the only Canadian member of the Science Fiction Writers of America.

Phyllis was born in Toronto in 1926 (as Phyllis Bloom). She attended the University of Toronto, receiving a B.A. in 1948 and an M.A. in 1950. In 1949, she married Calvin Gotlieb, now professor emeritus of Computer Science at University of Toronto. They have three grown children and four grandchildren. She lives in Toronto, her lifelong home.